War 1812

Remember
the
Raisin

Michael Aye

Published by Boson Books
An imprint of Bitingduck Press
Formerly an imprint of C&M Online Media, Inc.

ISBN 978-1-938463-11-2

For information contact
Bitingduck Press, LLC
Montreal • Altadena
notifications@bitingduckpress.com
http://www.bitingduckpress.com

Cover art by Dena Eaton
Image from "Tecumseh's death at the Battle of the Thames, with Colonel
Richard M. Johnson and the Kentucky mounted volunteers." Lithograph
by William Emmons, 1833.

Author's note
This book is a work of fiction with a historical backdrop. I have taken liberties with historical figures, ships, and time frames to blend in with my
story. Therefore, this book is not a reflection of actual historical events.

Books by Michael Aye

Fiction

The Reaper, Book One, The Fighting Anthonys
HMS SeaWolf, Book Two, The Fighting Anthonys
Barracuda, Book Three, The Fighting Anthonys
SeaHorse, Book Four, The Fighting Anthonys
Peregrine, Book Five, The Fighting Anthonys

Non-Fiction

What's the Reason for All That Wheezing and Sneezing
Michael A. Fowler and Nancy McKemie

In Memory of Tom
who was the catalyst for this trilogy

It's Your Heritage

Went to the courthouse, had to pay my tax
Flowing in the wind, I saw our country's flag
Suddenly I felt a change, a ghost within my soul
I was taken away, to a place I didn't know

...I heard the cannons roar
...Saw the soldiers stand
...Battle smoke filled the air
...Then I felt his hand

Take these colors, hold em high
Don't let 'em hit the ground
Gave my life protecting them
Don't you let 'em down

They've been shot and battle scarred
I think they've even bled
Carry them with pride, son
It's your heritage

Michael Aye

Prologue

"THEY'RE DEAD, EVERY LAST soul. *Kilt by the red devils. The Redcoats promised we'd be treated right if we surrendered but they let the injuns go plum wild. The red devils butchered every defenseless man, wounded or not. I barely survived. They were so busy scalping and tomahawking all the wounded soldiers that I was able to slip clean away. The British said they'd send wagons to collect all of us at one time; they lied. Instead, they let the injuns murder the lot of us, every loving mother's son. Most tried to get away but they couldn't. We didn't have no weapons to fight back with, they had been taken so the savages had easy pickens; like lambs to the slaughter. Kilt over a hundred I know. Most of the dead were fellow Kaintucks."*

Letting the man take a break to catch his breath, the major, commanding the small outpost, handed him a tankard of ale. The man was thirsty and hastily downed the liquid, nearly strangling as he did so. Then with tears coming to his eyes, he said, "Lost a lot of good friends, I did."

When the excited man calmed down, the major said, "Settle down, you are safe here. Now start over from the beginning. Tell me who you are."

The battered and ragged little man sat erect and seemed to get control of his emotions. "I'm Sergeant Monroe, sir. I was with General James Winchester's group; two thousand strong we was, when we started out from Kaintuck. Ain't many left now, I don't reckon. We was going to retake Fort Detroit. We were all part of General William Harrison's army. We retook Frenchtown. But the British General Proctor had about six hundred redcoats and eight hundred or so savages. During the night they flanked us. At sunrise, they attacked. That was January 22nd... I remember the date, cause it's my son's birthday." Pausing to take another sip of the ale,

Sergeant Monroe cleared his throat, and then continued, "Our General Winchester weren't much a soldier. He didn't put out near enough guards so there weren't no warning. Before we knowed it they were right on top of us. Chief Roundhead stripped the general naked and handed him over to the British." Shivering suddenly, Monroe seemed to be reliving the battle. "We fought till we plum give out of powder and ball. Major George Madison was the senior officer after Winchester got took. Proctor, the redcoat general, gave his word that if we surrendered, we'd be protected and our wounded taken care of decently. We, us Kaintucks, said we'd rather fight to the death. I wish we had, but someone sent up a white flag so that ended it... for the time being. I had an arrow in my wing and my noggin was creased by a ball so I got left behind with the wounded," Monroe said, emphasizing the bandages on his head and shoulder. "If me leg had been wounded where I couldn't have run and hid I wouldn't be here now. I'd be dead like the rest of 'em... God rest their souls. I reckon there were only about five hundred of us left able to fight anyway. Them that could walk were taken away as prisoners. Proctor was a'feard General Harrison would come back, so he up and left with the prisoners, and that is when the injuns started their devilish ways, robbing and tormenting our wounded. Soon they was killin' 'em outright, the bloodthirsty varmints. They's a trail strewn with American bodies where the red devils would finish butchering and scalping one, then run to another defenseless soul. Some of the wounded were burnt up in buildings the savages set afire. If I'd had a weapon, I'd done for a few of 'em, I would of. Don't ever trust them heathens, Major. Them Redcoats neither. If you get to thinking kindly toward the bunch, remember the River Raisin. Remember the massacre at the River Raisin."

Chapter One

H E WAS A TALL, bespectacled man with thinning hair combed over to hide a balding pate. It was a poor attempt. He was also a secretary to President James Madison. One would never expect this timid appearing man to speak with such a deep baritone and commanding voice. "The President will see you and... ahem, the gentleman now, Mr. Armstrong."

John Armstrong was a personal friend of the president. The man with him was Jonah Lee. Lee with Moses, his lifelong friend and protector, had ridden hard for several days, traveling from Georgia to arrive at this meeting with the president. He had arrived in Washington just in time to get into the coach with John Armstrong. The time of the meeting had not allowed Lee to freshen up or change his clothes. His three day growth of beard, rough appearance, and smell was reason for the secretary's ahem. What was it Moses had said, "I'd rather be down wind to a gut wagon than closed up in a room with you right now."

"John, how are you?" President Madison said in greeting to his friend.

"I am well, Mr. President. May I present Mr. Jonah Lee?"

"It's nice to meet you," Madison replied, shaking the extended grimy hand, his nostrils flaring in spite of his attempt at politeness.

"I apologize for my appearance, Mr. President," Lee started, but the apology was waved away.

"Nonsense, my good man, the needs of the nation outweighs niceties. John has convinced me you are the man to get things on track, so time is of the essence."

"I'm not sure I can meet the expectations that have been placed on me, sir, but I will give my all."

"I have no doubt," Madison responded. He liked the man right away. He could see why Lee had come so widely recommended by John Armstrong. His record with General Mad Anthony Wayne was almost a legend. Lee had been with Wayne at the Battle of Fallen Timbers. Though a youth of eighteen, Wayne placed a great deal of trust in Lee as a scout and advisor. During the battle Lee was said to have jumped between General Wayne and a Shawnee who was about to club Wayne from behind with a tomahawk. His rifle spent, Lee used it to block the Indian's chopping attack; and then he clubbed the savage with the butt plate. Another Indian was drawing back on his bowstring and Lee shot him with his pistol. The struggle was soon hand to hand but the Shawnee leader, Blue Jacket, realized the battle was lost and retreated with his braves.

Hoping for protection from Wayne's army, the Indians sought protection at Fort Miamis. With Lee and the other scouts leading the way, Wayne's army soon reached the fort. Fearing the American army, the British commander refused refuge for the Indians. The Indians soon realized that they were at a serious disadvantage fighting the Americans and a treaty was soon negotiated.

Wayne was quick to recognize the young Lee, not only for saving his life but also for his assistance during the campaign. "Lee is a man of courage and quick action," Wayne stated.

Thinking of the story, Madison gazed at the man standing in his travel stained clothes. It was not the soiled clothes that held his attention but the man... the hard man. His face was tanned and weathered from countless days outside in all kinds of weather. His chiseled face and rock of a jaw was scarred. His thick hair was prematurely gray, and his eyes were a cold blue. His six-foot frame seemed taller. A man most men would shy away from, but his rough masculine appearance would attract the women. He was, in short, a fighter. He would never be a diplomat. *But I don't need another diplomat*, Madison thought.

Viewing the man before him, Madison decided, *this is just what we need, a man of courage and quick action*. He rang for a servant and soon the three men sat down to coffee and pastries. Lee was most grateful. Because what food that had been consumed lately had been done so on the fly. Maybe it was his growling belly that prompted the president to order food.

"I'll not keep you long, Mr. Lee, I can see you are weary," Madison stated. "I'm sure John has told you of our failures, one after another. With the British policy of intercepting American ships, impressing our seamen, and stealing the ships' cargo we have been backed into a corner. That along with the demands of a "War Hawk Congress," we are immersed in a war we are poorly prepared to fight.

Lee munched hungrily at the pastries and watched as Madison stood and paced about while he spoke. "Damn Hull," he hissed. "Two blunders; two mind you. First, he included a letter detailing his plans for the invasion into Canada along with his personal baggage, heavier guns, and military stores. He knew the schooner he sent all this on had to pass Fort Malden. What was he thinking?" Madison outstretched his arms as if looking for a divine answer. After a pause, he continued, "Fort Malden is a British strong point. They captured the schooner, as one might expect along with Hull's papers, his supplies and even his sick men. If that's not enough, instead of pressing on, the…the damn fool laid over at the village of Sandwich, doing nothing, absolutely nothing, but let his army dwindle away that is. He had two thousand men… two thousand, mind you, when he started off. By the time Brock got there… now that's a mover and a fighter for you. British he may be but a fighter… blast him. Where was I, John?"

Apparently, Armstrong had heard the tirade before. "You were just getting to the British General Brock's attack, Mr. President."

"Yes. Well, Brock, from all reports, didn't have but maybe three hundred regulars when he arrived at Amherstburg. However, there he met up with that Indian, Tecumseh, who is chief of the Shawnee. Tecumseh had seven hundred or so warriors. The two forces teamed up, and then rounded up some four hundred militias...a sizeable force, but not one that couldn't be dealt with. Now, to make matters worse, Hull was more worried about a supply convoy than he was about being attacked." This Madison said looking up and rolling his eyes. "He sent about four hundred men to find a supply convoy. That left him only eight hundred and fifty or so men to defend his position when Brock attacked. But, he still held a good position. That evening... August fifteenth, I believe," Madison said, gazing over to Armstrong, who gave a slight nod confirming the date.

Seeing the nod, Madison continued, "Brock asked Hull to surrender, which he refused. When a lucky cannon ball hit the officer's mess, killing four men, the next morning at breakfast, Hull ran up the white flag. The coward! Not only did he surrender Detroit's fort and town, the fool included the four hundred or so men he sent out after the supply convoy. In his report, Hull stated he feared the Indians would run rampant and slaughter his soldiers."

Picking up a sheet of paper, Madison continued, "Hull's surrender meant the British captured one thousand six hundred Ohio volunteers, five hundred eighty-two American regulars, thirty-three cannons, two thousand five hundred muskets, and the brig, *Adams*."

Letting the paper fall back on top of his desk, Madison took a swallow of his coffee, paused then asked with disgust in his voice, "Mr. Lee, can you guess how many casualties were suffered?"

"No sir, Mr. President."

"Four, sir; the four officers killed eating their breakfast. Four. The British had no casualties. Not so much as a scratch. We lose a fort, a town, and enough supplies to equip an army for months, not to mention the momentum to invade Canada. All without inflicting one single casualty. The man is a coward, Mr. Lee. I'll see him court-martialed if we ever get him back from the British."

Lee had remained quiet during the president's tirade. There had been little interaction between the men as the president gave little inclination any was desired.

Madison gave a deep sigh; he appeared tired and exhausted after his comments. Picking up his coffee cup, Madison drained the remainder of the lukewarm coffee, setting the cup down so hard it clanked on the saucer. Madison remained silent for a moment as he seemed to be in deep thought. Finally, after another sigh, he continued, "I'm sure you've been informed about the massacre at Frenchtown, or as some are calling it, the River Raisin."

"Yes sir," Lee answered. "Couriers have spread the word."

"Yes, I'm sure they have," Madison responded dejectedly. "Bad news travels like wildfire. At least they made a battle of it at the Raisin. Unlike Hull, they fought until they ran out of ammunition. Now we've a rally cry. Proctor made a mistake letting the Indians butcher our people. I want to make the most of that mistake." Madison then walked tiredly back to his desk, opened a drawer and pulled out a paper. He turned toward Lee and spoke again. "Mr. Lee, you are to see we push forward. You are a man of action and I want you to push. Push our generals to act. Push hard if need be. General William Henry Harrison has replaced Hull. He's no coward but he's cautious… cautious to a fault. You are to push him to act, even if it takes a swift kick in the pants. He must push forward before winter or all is lost."

Handing Lee the paper, Madison said, "This document signed by me requires everyone to extend whatever support you may require. I'd prefer you not flourish it about, as that would cause jealousy and hard feelings by some. However, should the need arise, use it. Use it and I'll stand by you."

Seeing Madison gaze at a clock, Armstrong and Lee recognized their time with the president was over. As they made ready to leave, Madison spoke again, "Mr. Lee, this war needs strong leaders if we are to win. I, above all, recognize that. Just as John places an extreme confidence in you, I also place that same confidence in him. I tell you this so you will not be surprised when you hear that he will soon be made Secretary of War."

Lee smiled, finally feeling the freedom to speak openly, and said, "A wise choice, if I may say so, Mr. President... a wise choice."

Chapter Two

THE GATHERING ROOM WAS full of men in heated conversation about the war. Some were blaming Madison and the Congress for getting "us" into this war. While others gave the war staunch support... "We cannot tolerate such high-handed ways. Specially, after the way Proctor let our men be slaughtered by those heathens at the River Raisin. We have got to give 'em war."

Outside, a cold east wind blew as raindrops pattered on the tavern's front windows. Jonah Lee and his fellow traveler, Moses, made themselves comfortable in a corner of the tavern at a table situated not far from the fireplace. It was a snug place and the promise of a room upstairs with a "passable" bed was enough to keep the men holed up for the night. Moses had caused more than one of the men to take a look at him as they warmed themselves at the fireplace.

The tavern keeper had considered telling Moses that he'd have to sleep in the stable but a quick glance at Jonah Lee was enough for the man to hold his tongue. Anyone else who didn't like the arrangements...well they were free to bring it up with Mr. Lee. A few glared but no one spoke.

The country was sparsely settled, and those who settled rarely traveled out of the county. To see a man of color was strange indeed. Moses was what some would call a mixed breed. His father had been a runaway slave, and his mother a Creek Indian. He'd been named Moses by his father after hearing where the biblical Moses had led his people out of bondage to the promised land.

Moses would probably have been raised as an Indian had not the village people all died from the smallpox. Moses bore the scars of the disease on his face to this day. He was twelve summers, half-starved and dehydrated when Jonah's father found him. He'd taken the boy home, nursed him back to life and he'd lived with the family ever since. Jonah had been seven then and amazed by the sudden addition to the family. Moses' skin color was that of a light-skinned black but his hair was straight like his mother's people. He had been able to grow a scraggly beard which helped to cover the scars on his face. The beard was now salt and pepper as shades of gray crept into it. So far his hair, which was shaggy but didn't reach his shoulders, was still black. Until the tragedy of the smallpox wiping out his village, Moses had been raised to be a warrior. His grandfather had taken particular interest in his upbringing. That interest had paid off well over time. Through the years, Moses had imparted a lot of his knowledge to Jonah. Raised to-gether as boys, they'd been inseparable as men. Moses had been with Jonah as one of General "Mad" Anthony Wayne's scouts.

After the war, things had gotten to the point of being monotonous when Jonah had been summoned by his friend, John Armstrong. They had just returned from a trip down into Florida when the letter had been delivered by an old soldier delivering mail astride a swayback mule. The grizzled toothless old pensioner spit a stream of tobacco juice that hit one of Lee's barking cur dogs on the head. The dog ran off a piece, turned and started barking again until Jonah quieted him.

"Got cha a letter here from Washington," the man offered as he handed down the mail. "Spec you'll be gallivanting off somewhere soon. Wished I was younger, I'd jine up and put a lickin' on them red-coats like we did last war." Jonah and Moses couldn't help but smile at the fire in the old man's voice.

After a few days of rest in Washington, Jonah and Moses had resumed their journey, this time to meet up with General Harrison. They were now entering the Ohio frontier.

The smell of cooked beans and pork filled the air in the tavern and Jonah's stomach growled. A group of men dressed in buckskins sat at a large center table. They had their pipes lit and were drinking rum like there was no tomorrow. One of the men seemed to stand out from the others. He wore the same buckskins and moccasins, but he was different. It finally dawned on Jonah... it was his speech. His speech was that of an educated man. It was not long before one of the men addressed him as captain. *These are Kentuckians*, Jonah realized. He'd met others like this group before. Hard drinking, hard fighting men who had a gift for telling you a tall-tale in a second. Their tales were so outrageous, they'd break down in laughter before the tale was finished. But they were also woodsmen and deadly shots with their weapons. Jonah doubted that they could be equaled when it came to marksmanship. These brawling, swaggering men carried long rifles so accurate that they could hit a nail's head as far as it could be seen. They were only a dozen or so of them but they'd make an impact regardless of their number.

A bowl of steaming hot beans and a platter of pork with fresh baked bread and a pot of molasses were set at their table. Jonah ordered more ale for the two of them and as he and Moses dug in, he decided that he would talk to the Kentucky leader in the morning. It might be they were headed in the same direction and could travel together. But tonight, it was food and then bed.

"Think we ought to crack a window?" Moses asked as the door was closed on their room.

"Why," Jonah responded. "It's a terrible night out."

"I just don't want it to be a terrible night in," Moses replied. "Those beans are sure to start working on your innards."

"Well, if they do, there's no cause for concern because my gas smells like roses."

"Yeah," Moses said, cutting his eyes and opening the window a crack. "They smell like roses...dead roses."

One of the servant girls was sweeping the stone floor the next morning when Jonah and Moses came down. A small fire still burned in the fireplace to take the chill out of the gathering room. The mixed aroma of coffee, bacon, and biscuits filled the room. The sun was rising, and the day promised to be a good one. The door opened as one of the Kentuckians entered. His eyes were swollen as a result of last night's heavy drinking. He, nevertheless, smiled at Jonah, "It's gonna be a scorcher, friend."

The whinny of a horse was heard outside. *He's seen to the caring of the group's horses*, Jonah thought. As if reading Jonah's thoughts, Moses volunteered, "I'd better go see to ours."

Breakfast was a fast paced affair. The travelers who had taken refuge from the wet and dreary night were ready to be on their way before it got hot.

The leader of the group of Kentuckians was a man named Clay Gesslin. He was a militia captain and was leading his group to join up with others from his area already under General Harrison's command.

"We stayed behind till the crops were laid in, then we came on," Clay volunteered over breakfast. "Now we're going to join Colonel Johnson and the rest of our men."

"It could be we might travel together," Jonah said as the men shook hands. "We are headed that way ourselves."

"If you've a mind to and you can keep up, you're welcome," Clay responded. "We intend to push hard. We don't want the fighting to be over and done with before we get there," he said with a smile.

Thinking of the men's partying last night; Jonah could tell just how big a rush they were in. After breakfast, Jonah and Moses packed their belongings in bed rolls and saddled up to leave. Thanking the owner of the tavern for his good service, the men paid their bill and rode off together in one group.

The so-called road soon turned into little more than a path through the woods. Due to the previous night's rain, the path turned into a succession of bog holes. Soon the horses were slipping up to their withers in the bogs.

"Damned if we near couldn't nah done better with a boat than these horses," one man complained as he was pitched from his saddle as his horse slipped down. Seeing the horse was having trouble rising up, the man picked up his hat as he walked over to the animal raking a clump of mud off his shoulder as he did so. Reaching the horse, the man cursed loudly, "Damn this here road, damn those Redcoats and damn this horse. He's done broke his leg."

Retrieving his saddle and belongings from the horse he handed them to a friend on horseback. Taking a pistol from his belt, the man walked back to his horse. Watching, Jonah could see tears on the fellow's face as he spoke softly to the animal before he shot it. No sooner had the echo of the shot died away when Clay said, "Move out."

The group continued on the path, passing fewer and fewer homesteads as they traveled. Frightened homeowners peered out of windows or doorways that were cracked open just enough to see through. The conspicuous barrel of a musket always evident, letting the travelers know the settlers were ready to defend their property if need be. At the first couple of cabins, the men tried to buy a horse but were told there was none to be spared. At the second cabin, a man braver than most opened the door to talk with the group.

Jonah could feel the hairs on the back of his neck stand up. Even though he couldn't see anyone he had the feeling they were covered; probably from the barn or from the loft in the cabin. The man had stated there was a tavern and trading post down at the end of the road a piece. It was at the edge of the wilderness and an animal might be purchased there. The remark he made about at the edge of the wilderness made Jonah laugh. He felt he had been in the wilderness for most of the day. Had their land been much as this area was when his father had decided to settle there? He'd often said he'd hacked out a homestead. His words had a new meaning to Jonah now that he was able to see and old enough to understand his father's meaning. He had always respected his father but now that respect grew.

The sun was going down when the group rode into a clearing. In the center of the clearing was a tavern and trading post with a covered walkway to a barn and a corral just past the barn. A man stacking firewood paused, and pushing his hat back he watched as the group rode into the clearing and stopped. Jonah and Captain Gesslin introduced themselves.

"Light and sit," the man said. "Supper is near done. Besides you can't go much further tonight. The trail gets rough and near impassable at places. You may even consider taking the river from here on."

Inside, the tavern lamps had already been lit. The place had a high ceiling with smoky beams. From the beams, lamps were suspended on ropes so they could be raised and lowered to be lit or be put out as needed. The windows were fitted with shutters that could be opened or closed from the inside. Each of the shutters had a cross cut into it for firing guns. The walls of the tavern were at least two feet thick and made out of stone. The place was a fortress of sorts; impregnable to anything less than cannon. The roof may burn but nothing else would.

As the men washed away the mud and grime from the road, two women went about setting the tables. Probably mother and daughter, Jonah decided. The meal was a virtual feast. As the men had not stopped to eat since breakfast it was a much welcome sight. The owner of the tavern had addressed the older of the two women as Mary when he told her the men would be staying over. With the help of the younger girl, Mary brought food to the tables. First she brought out two pots of beans with a mixture of chopped cucumbers and onions. Two haunches of roasted venison followed, then brown bread still hot from the oven. The young girl set small tubs of freshly churned butter, along with jars of canned blackberry preserves, as well as mincemeat pie and a creamy cheese made from sour milk. Homemade beer and ale was also in the offering for drink. The men ate heartily and went to bed early, exhausted from the day's ordeal. Tomorrow was soon enough to decide about continuing on horseback or possibly taking to the river as the proprietor had recommended.

Chapter Three

THE WIND WAS DRIVING from the east, and the rain that had disappeared yesterday seemed likely to return today. Jonah doused water on his face and felt the early morning fog in his head clear. By the time a breakfast of fatback and biscuits with cups of strong black coffee had been finished, the sound of crows cawing and squabbling over what little morsel of food their neighbor had found could be heard. Following the tavern owner down to the river, Jonah saw the man's wife giving an Indian squaw with a couple of small children food. They had gone to the back door to keep from startling any of the tavern's guests.

"They're friendly," the man said by way of explanation. "I give them leftovers, and they give me trinkets of various sorts. We can take them down to the village and sell a few now and again."

"I wouldn't be giving them any rum," Captain Gesslin volunteered.

"Naw, we don't trade any of that. It's just the squaws trading with the misses. We don't get many braves about."

"Probably off fighting alongside the Redcoats." This was from one of Gesslin's men.

As the men made their way to the river's edge, one of the men placed his moccasin clad foot on the bow of a birch wood canoe, and the canoe turned over. The man seemed to fidget about and then turned to Gesslin and spoke.

"Captain, if it's all the same to you, I'd as soon keep traveling on my hoss. I can't swim a lick and this here... boat seems a might frail to me." The man's concerns were enough to set the others to joshing him.

"What you so skittish for, 'fraid you might get dumped into the river? Well, it'd probably do you some good was you to have a bar of soap handy."

"Hush up, Hicks, I took a bath during the summer, same as you."

"Shore you did," Hicks declared. "Only I've had one a month since."

This caused more laughter until Gesslin broke it up. "I'm inclined to agree with Lang. I don't mind fishing out of a boat, but when it comes to fighting, I'd rather have my horse beneath me."

This brought a chorus of agreement from the men. Jonah gave a slight nod to Moses and he went to pack up. This was the last known tavern and trading post until they reached Franklinton; so Jonah and Gesslin bought more supplies. Moses had their packs together in a matter of minutes. In one, he packed coffee, a slab of bacon, salt, a small bag of flour and one bag of cornmeal. Even adding the new purchases to their supplies it was still mighty slim provisions for the trip ahead. They would have to live off the land and fish when they could.

Getting his gear together, Jonah laid a couple of woolen shirts and a pair of woolen socks down on his blanket then rolled it up. That way they'd be handy if he got wet or it turned cold. The early September morning already had a chill. Tying his blanket roll on the back of his saddle, Jonah watched as Moses checked the patch boxes and shot pouches. Their rifles would be useless without patches and shot. He then wrapped a couple of extra flints in a small rag and placed them in the patch box. With their powder horns full and each of them having an additional horn tied to their saddles, they were ready. Leading their horses over to where the Kentuckians were standing, loud voices could be heard.

Captain Gesslin was haggling over the price of a horse with the tavern owner. He felt the owner had intended to sell them the canoes or trade them for their horses with the promise they could pick them up or buy them back on the return trip. Trouble was, it was unlikely they would come back this way anytime soon. Therefore, the horses would be the man's to do with as he pleased. It would be easy to sell the horses and say they were stolen. A deal was finally struck after the tavern owner noticed the Kentuckians had circled about him with a no-nonsense glare in their eyes. The man still got a better than fair price for the horse but grumbled he'd been robbed. The grumbling stopped suddenly under the glare of Gesslin's men.

The sun was bright and starting to warm up as they headed out following the west bank of the Scioto River. Riding close to the river was difficult in places, so they followed game trails as they were able, always keeping close to the river. At places the trails widened and looked well traveled. Jonah felt these trails were likely used by Indians. The path wound crookedly along the edge of the woods. They were steadily climbing as they went when Captain Gesslin halted his horse suddenly. The rest of the men reacted as one forming a wedge-like formation with the group on either side of the captain looking toward the woods and listening.

"I smell smoke," Moses whispered to Jonah.

After pausing, the group rode on slowly keeping their guns ready. The climb leveled off on a small rise and faint tendrils of smoke drifted on the breeze as it filtered through the tall dark pines. The captain halted abruptly and got down from his saddle, giving the reins to the man behind him who still sat on his horse. Watching from his horse, Jonah could see Gesslin as he eased through the woods, until he disappeared from sight. The men sat in their saddles for what seemed like an eternity, tense and alert. The drifts of smoke and the deathly silence created an eerie sensation.

The horses seemed uneasy as first one then another would paw the ground then blow. Gesslin finally came back in sight and waved for them to come forward. A clearing of several acres opened up as they rode forward. A small stream ran from the river past a cabin and outbuildings. What used to be a cabin was not much more than smoldering embers at this point. The settlers had been attacked yesterday from the look of things. It appeared the family had been massacred as they went about their daily chores with little or no warning. A man lay next to a well with an arrow sticking from between his shoulders and one in his neck. A youth… a boy of about sixteen, lay next to a lean-to with his head a bloody black pulp.

"They took a tomahawk to him," one of Gesslin's men volunteered.

By the cabin door a naked woman lay dead. The dried blood between her legs was evidence she had been raped. Both breasts had been cut off.

"Hope she was dead when they did that," Moses said as he picked up a bedspread that lay nearby and draped it over the corpse.

A call from the barn startled Jonah. They walked over to where one of the Kentuckians was standing. A teenage girl had been wrapped in a cowhide which was dangling from a rafter by a rope. The girl's eyes had been punctured, the sticks still in place. Like the other woman, her breasts were gone also. The man, whose name was Hicks, cut the leather lace binding the cowhide together, and they could see the girl had been tied up. She couldn't use her hands to remove the sticks. She had been raped as well.

"She's still breathing," one of the men said in disbelief.

As the rope binding her was cut, she whispered, "Kill me… kill me, please."

Jonah was shocked when Gesslin took his razorback from its scabbard and deftly sliced the tortured girl's throat. Jonah wanted to be angry but realized it was a kindness. *Would I have been able to do it*, he wondered.

Looking at Moses, he nodded his agreement with what Gesslin had done as he turned from the scene. Looking about the yard, several empty and broken clay jugs of rum were found. Jonah kicked a half-burned blanket aside and found a pouch full of tobacco.

"They overlooked that," Moses said.

Jonah handed the leather pouch to his friend for safekeeping. They both enjoyed a bowl of the devil's weed when the opportunity to light their pipes arose. On the other side of the lean-to flies buzzed around the carcass of the cow the Indians had skinned to use the hide on the girl. As the green skin dried, it would tighten on the girl until she couldn't breathe... a slow death.

"Those were a torturing bunch of heathens," Moses volunteered.

Not knowing if they were being watched or not they made a quick job of burying the family. Nosing around while some of the men were digging the graves Jonah and Moses found a small cellar with several jars of canned foods. The woman had done a right smart job of canning in preparation for the hard winter ahead. The men took what they could carry and then with little more than a prayer they left the buried bodies without the benefit of a cross. The group had been there no more than an hour when they made their way back to the trail.

They rode until dark and then made camp. While some of the men tended to the horses, others went about preparing the campsite. A couple of small fires were made to make coffee and heat up some of the canned goods they had found. The fires were well banked so the blazes were not visible from beyond a few feet. Making a few small fires was better than a large blaze which would have created too much of a glow. Moses spread his and Jonah's bedrolls on a pile of pine needles next to a gigantic old pine tree. As Jonah lay down, he pulled his blanket up over him as there was a chill in the air. *It will come a frost soon,* he thought. Lying there in the quiet, he could hear the river as the water flowed. Before morning, the sound of an animal walking down to the water to drink woke Jonah up. The chatter of a couple of boar coons fighting made several of the men rise up from their blankets until each had identified the sound. Satisfied no Indians were about, they rolled over and went back to sleep.

Jonah had volunteered himself and Moses' services to stand watch, but Gesslin said they had a routine down and didn't want to break it. The thought was appreciated but not needed. Jonah wondered if Gesslin didn't trust them as woodsmen yet.

Seeing Jonah's look of concern, Gesslin quickly dispelled that idea. "We have a system," he said. "There's no need to change. The men know each other and who relieves whom and where they bed down."

When the gray light of false dawn appeared the men got up and started stirring about camp. The ground had been cold even through the pine needles and ground blanket. Jonah awoke with a dull ache and stiffness in his back. Watching some of the others stretch, he realized he wasn't the only one the cold, hard ground had gotten too. Of course, they hadn't had a fire of any size to help with the cold either.

In half an hour, the men had their fill of coffee and bacon. They had finished what bread they had brought. They would have to make pan bread from now on if bread was to be had. One of the men had walked to the river's edge to wash the frying pan and rinse out the coffee pot. He had no sooner gotten out of sight when he rushed back into camp.

"Injuns," he hissed. "Several large canoes full of the devils."

"How far?" Gesslin asked.

"In sight." By that, he meant they'd made it around the bend in the river and were on the straightway. That meant they were no more than one hundred fifty yards and probably less.

Gesslin called to one of his men to secure the horses; so they wouldn't break loose if it came to a fight. The fires had been put out a good fifteen minutes ago so there was no smoke but the unmistakable smell of cooked bacon and wood smoke hung heavy in the early morning air. Jonah had seen Gesslin send a man to the river to keep watch. He was back now.

Jonah heard him tell Gesslin in a hushed voice, "There are five canoes with four or five warriors in each. They all had on war paint." One, he noticed, had on an army coat.

It could have been picked up anywhere or anytime, Jonah thought, *maybe even from the burned out settler's cabin.* The most important part of the man's report was that they were closing in toward the bank on our side of the river.

"Looks like we're in for a fight," Moses whispered as he handed Jonah his long rifle.

Without another word, they all spread out. Picking their belongings off the ground, the men found cover for themselves. The area wouldn't stand a close inspection but from a distance all looked as it should be. The smell was what lured them in, Jonah was sure. The Indians landed and drew their canoes high on the river bank, moving silently through the trees to where the camp had been.

The men crouched, waiting, as the Indians inched forward making their way around small saplings and briars. Jonah's group waited, hoping and praying the horses wouldn't make a sound. Jonah had grown up in and around the woods. His father had taken Moses and him hunting from the time he was able to pick up a gun. Later, it was just Moses and Jonah supplying most of the meat for the table. Jonah's father preferred deer over cow any day. However, all the hunting Jonah had done for wild game was nothing compared to hunting a man.

He'd learned the hard way when he was with General Wayne's scouts. The snap of a twig under his arm as he raised his rifle had caused a swarm of Indians to attack him once. Luckily, the other scouts had been there.

Now Jonah waited and watched. He could feel his heartbeat, but he was not nervous. As the Indians moved closer, each cautious step brought them a little closer to the trap. Suddenly, a brave raised his bow to fire. He died before the arrow was fully drawn back. The sudden explosion of gunfire left half of the Indians down and kicking.

The Kentuckians rushed from their cover with Jonah and Moses along with them. One brave hacked at Jonah with a tomahawk. He parried it easily with his rifle then butted the Indian with the brass butt plate. For a moment, the hand to hand fighting was intense. However, half the Indians had been dropped with their volley. Moses was in a crouched position as a brave circled with him. Once the brave got a little closer, Jonah laid the barrel of his rifle against the warrior's head, splitting the upper ear and scalp. The brave yelped in pain, went down on all four but came up quickly running for the river. Three more braves followed after him. The rest were down, some were dead, and others were just wounded.

Jonah did a quick count. Every one of the Kentuckians was accounted for with no apparent serious injury.

"Moses," Jonah called. "Come with me."

They ran down to the river but were too late to catch the retreating Indians. Four Indians were paddling a canoe hard, their arms rising and dipping as they headed down river. They were already too far for a good shot, so the two men went back to the campsite. The dead Indians had been stretched out together. The more seriously wounded were left lying, and those with minor wounds were bound loosely. They would break free soon, after Jonah's group had broken camp and pulled out. They could attend to their own then.

In less than half an hour, the men had packed their blanket rolls, saddled their horses and were on their way. The sun peeking over the trees sent rays of sunlight through the forest. Jonah had never run from a fight, but looking back at the dead bodies and thinking about the settlers they had buried yesterday, he thought... *what a waste. Will it always be so? Surely men would look back at history and not repeat the same mistakes. Or would they?*

It seemed as if Moses was reading Jonah's mind or following his gaze. "It's been like this since David's time," he said. *Moses would know,* Jonah thought. He was a man who knew the scriptures.

Chapter Four

THE REMAINDER OF THE trip to Franklinton was uneventful. They passed a couple of small parties of Indians, but they were not wearing war paint. One party even had a few squaws and small children in it, so there was little to fear from them. It was late... almost nine p.m. when they came to the outskirts of the town.

Despite the lateness, the men were all satisfied that they'd decided to press on since dawn. Arriving in town tonight meant not having to spend another cold night on the trail and worrying about Indian attacks. The men must have looked a sight as they walked their horses down Gift Street. Although there were a few people stirring, most of the houses were dark as folks had already gone to bed. A dozen heavily armed men riding into town was enough to cause the few people who were still up to stop and take note.

They rode on briefly stopping at a livery stable long enough to find out if there were any soldiers in town, and if so, where they could be located. They left the livery stable and headed down Broad Street. As they rode in the direction where the army was camped, they passed a jail and a courthouse.

Gesslin turned in the saddle and spoke to his men, "You men keep civil while we are here. I don't want to have to come looking for you at either of those places."

This brought a couple of laughs and snickers as Gesslin knew it would. He then turned to Jonah and spoke, "You probably don't know it, Jonah, but it was a Kentuckian who built this town. Fellow named Lucas Sullivant. He was a surveyor. He was sent to survey the Scioto

River. Afterwards, he was given several thousand acres as reward for his trouble. Part of what is called the Scioto River Basin. He first laid out his town starting at the riverbanks. Then the rains came and flooded the proposed town site. That didn't bother him much though. He just started over, moving the town about a mile away. To bring in folks, he gave away plots to anyone willing to build a house on a certain street. It was named Gift Street. That's the one we rode in on. Since then, he's got hitched. Now he's done built his wife a fine new brick house. He also built her a church, and some say a school is in the making. Now, other folks, land speculators and such, are pushing a new town just up the road. They call it Columbus. Lots more money involved, so I wouldn't be surprised to hear that Franklinton just dried up or got swept aside for this new town. Don't seem right though. Not after all Sullivant did for the place."

"You seem to be well informed," Jonah said.

"I should be. I was one of a group of twenty men Sullivant brought up from Kentucky to survey the river. That was back in 1795. He offered me the same deal of free land to build on. Said it was to honor Ben Franklin, but I wanted to head back home. I figured I'd let others have the pleasure of honoring old Ben." Turning in his saddle, Gesslin spoke to the men. "Here we are, fellows."

The group pulled up in front of a brick building with a sign that read, Sullivant Land Office. A uniformed sentry stood watch at the front door of the building. Tents and campfires were visible in the field behind the building. The door of the building opened before they could address the sentry. A tall man with a glass in his hand opened the door and stepped outside. The sentry came to attention.

The man stared at the group for a moment then spoke, "Damn, Clay, took you long enough. I figured you'd either gotten lost or had your hair parted."

Smiling, Gesslin dismounted and shaking the man's hand said, "Well, there was a few who tried it."

After shaking hands, Gesslin introduced Jonah, "Colonel Johnson, this is Jonah Lee. Lee, this is the best soldier in all of Kentucky... Colonel Richard Mentor Johnson."

Dismounting, Lee shook hands with the colonel. After the greeting and introductions were complete, the sentry was sent to fetch a sergeant who took the rest of the Kentuckians to find a campsite. Moses looked at Jonah who gave a slight nod. They had come this far with the group, so they'd camp with them tonight. Jonah would find out from Johnson where he might find General Harrison. But that could wait until tomorrow. Thus far, the President's paper remained unused. How long would it remain so?

Jonah liked Johnson immediately, as he had Clay Gesslin, but he didn't want to reveal his hand as yet. Some people would act much differently when they think they are on equal ground, compared to someone seen as having more authority.

Tonight, and perhaps over the next day or so, Jonah wanted to get to know Johnson's thoughts and feelings, as well as other men in leadership positions, as to how the war was coming along. Jonah didn't want to be underhanded, but he'd been given an assignment by the President. He now had to do the best job he could, the best way he could find.

The next morning after breakfast Jonah was talking with Gesslin and Colonel Johnson when a messenger arrived. General Clay's scouts had spotted the British army under General Proctor. The army also had a large number of Shawnee braves under Tecumseh with them. Hearing this, Colonel Johnson gave orders to break camp and move out. Johnson had approximately one thousand men under his command at this point. Being mounted men, they would move quickly but not near as fast as Jonah felt he and Moses could move being unhampered by wagons, cannons, supplies and such.

As the army under Johnson prepared to mobilize, Jonah decided he and Moses would push on ahead. Shaking hands with Gesslin, Jonah bid him farewell with the hopes that they'd meet again up north. He had come to like the lanky Kentuckian very much. With soldiers like him, the Americans would be hard to beat.

The horses were worn out after being pushed hard. Jonah and Moses rode into Camp Seneca as the sun was setting in the western sky. Even that late in the day the camp was a bustle of activity. At the edge of the camp, Jonah and Moses were challenged by a sentry, who, after being told who they were, called for the sergeant of the guard. Waiting on the sergeant, the man became very talkative.

"Orders, you know. Everybody has to be escorted into the camp... been a heap-o-killin' lately. Red devils sneaking up on people all up and down the river; butchering folks and taking their scalps. Man, woman, youngun... makes no difference to them savages. You can't be sure what's going to happen next," the man said as he spit a stream of tobacco juice. He started to speak again but was interrupted by the sergeant.

Jonah introduced himself and said he was here to see General Harrison.

"Lots of folks want to see the general," the sergeant responded sarcastically. "Not many of them do, however."

"I'm here on assignment," Jonah replied.

"You don't look like no soldier to me," the sergeant said.

"I'm not."

"I thought you just said you'd been assigned."

Not wanting to lose his temper with the man, Jonah asked, "Is there an officer about?"

"Shore they is. That don't mean you gonna see him either. He's eating his supper bout now, I reckon."

That did it. Dropping the reins to his horse, Jonah stepped forward so fast the sergeant stumbled backing up. "Sergeant, if you want to keep those stripes you better have me in front of the duty officer fast."

Realizing he'd likely made a blunder but trying to save face in front of the sentry, the sergeant said, "Have your man wait here and you follow me."

Jonah realized why the sergeant had said what he did but cared little for the man's bruised authority at this moment. "I tell my man where to go, Sergeant, not you. Now move out."

Without being told, Moses took the reins to Jonah's horse and followed. As he passed the sentry, he was not surprised to see a big smile on the man's tobacco stained face. *Probably had more than his share of bullying from the sergeant,* Moses thought.

The duty officer was more cordial than the sergeant. He shook hands with Jonah and offered him and Moses a cup of coffee and stated he'd inquire when the general might see them.

Fearing he was about to be put off again, Jonah said, "Tell the general we are here from Washington." He'd not used the President's name, but the captain was sure to understand the implication.

Jonah was not sure how General Harrison would receive them but doubted they'd have long before they found out. He was right. The captain was back before the cup of coffee had been finished. The coffee was good and helped ease the weariness from the hard ride. Draining the cup, Jonah would like to have had another cup of the strong black liquid. Maybe the general would offer him one.

Moses made to rise, but Jonah said, "Stay and rest, old friend, I'm sure the captain has more coffee and will find something for you to eat while you wait. That won't be any problem, will it, Captain?" Jonah addressed the officer, letting him know this was more than a mere request. He expected Moses to be taken care of in his absence.

General Harrison was going over a set of maps when Jonah was ushered into his tent. Turning to see who entered, Harrison rose, a smile on his face. "By all that's holy, if it's not Jonah Lee. Are you the man from Washington?"

Jonah also had a smile on his face as he responded, "Guilty."

"Well... sit down, sit down. Would you prefer a glass of wine, a cup of coffee... or something stronger," Harrison asked.

"Coffee will do, sir," Jonah replied.

He noticed a slight nod from the captain, who'd been going over the maps with the general. Obviously, he'd passed a test.

Harrison turned to the captain and spoke, "Hammond, the man you see before you saved the life of General Wayne at Fallen Timbers. He was a young man then... we both were. I was Wayne's aide-de-camp, and Jonah was Wayne's most trusted scout. Neither of us had reached our twentieth year, as I recall. I was nineteen," Harrison said then looked at Jonah.

"I was eighteen," Jonah added.

Harrison made his way to a handmade chair behind the rough table the map was spread across. "You've been sent by Madison to spy on me, haven't you?"

Taken aback by Harrison's remark, Jonah took a sip of coffee, thereby giving him time to frame his response. "More like to add assistance and support," he said.

Harrison nodded then replied, "You're a damn good liar, Jonah, never-the-less I'm glad to see you and have you with us."

"Thank you, General," Jonah answered and realized that he meant it.

Chapter Five

REPORTS CAME IN DAILY of minor excursions along the upper and lower Sandusky. It appeared the British had given up any attempt to gain possession of the Maumee Valley and Fort Meigs for the time being. However, the Indians struck at every chance, attacking small patrols and supply convoys. Tecumseh, the Shawnee chief, continued with these sudden raids, spreading alarm throughout the extreme northwest section of Ohio. Jonah and Moses rode with Captain Clay Gesslin as he took out a patrol along the Sandusky. Moses was starting to get grumpy hanging around the camp all day, drinking kill devil and playing cards at night. Truth be told Jonah had gotten restless himself and was afraid he was making a nuisance of himself around headquarters. The opportunity to ride out on patrol was a welcome change.

"They tell me," Gesslin said, "that Colonel Johnson and his regiment is starting to get impatient doing nothing but riding patrols."

"I hear," Gesslin continued after shifting in his saddle so he'd be facing Jonah as they talked, "that we are soon to make a sweep of Indian country then rendezvous at Fort Winchester. The rumor is a fleet is being assembled to battle the British on Lake Erie. If they are successful, we are to move against Malden and hopefully retake Detroit. There is even talk we may try to take York."

Jonah was not sure if his friend's words were being informative or if he was asking about the truth of the rumor. After a pause, Jonah finally said, "That's my understanding, as well."

Any further comments on the subject were halted when a point rider galloped his horse toward the group. The horse came to a sudden halt, blowing to catch a breath; its chest heaved as the animal pawed the ground and blew hard from its efforts.

The scout was excited and had to take deep breaths before he could speak. "It's the... whole... army, the whole British army, Captain."

"You're sure?" Gesslin asked.

"Yes... sir. They's between two and three thousand redcoats and just as many of the red devils. I saw Tecumseh with my own eyes... seen that British general, too. Least I think he was a general. He had on enough gold to feed all of Kaintuck for a year or more."

"Could you tell where they were heading?" Gesslin asked.

"Toward Fort Meigs I'd say, Captain."

"We've got to find a way to warn the fort," Jonah said breaking his silence.

"I don't reckon that would be possible, Mr. Lee," the scout advised. "They's so spread out by the time you worked your way clear, they'd already be at the fort."

Jonah had no doubt the man's words were true. Besides, Fort Meigs was commanded by General Clay. He was a most capable man. There would be little doubt he didn't have pickets posted to warn him of any attack.

"What other fort is near?" Jonah asked.

Gesslin opened his leather map case and pulled a worn paper from it. "I'd say Fort Stephenson," he responded after looking at his map.

"Then that's where Moses and I will head, Clay. They need to know the British are out in force."

Jonah could see his friend was torn between going back to General Harrison's camp, and riding on to Fort Stephenson. Suddenly, the decision was made for him. A shot rang out and a man fell from his saddle as another man shouted, "Injuns."

"Into the trees," Gesslin ordered.

Once off the trail, Gesslin dismounted his horse. Grabbing the reins of Jonah's horse, he shouted to be heard above the gunfire and war cries. "Ride, Jonah, we'll hold them off, and if possible, we'll follow."

Knowing what the odds were, Jonah said, "I'll buy the first round at Fort Stephenson, Clay."

Turning their nervous horses and riding low in the saddle, Moses and Jonah galloped away amid the din of the growing battle. Jonah was tempted to send Moses on and return but knew one more man would mean little in the fight. Besides, Fort Stephenson's commander would heed his warnings far quicker than he would Moses.

"May God be with you, Clay," Jonah prayed as they rode on.

"Riders coming," a sentry called out.

Lieutenant Shipp approached the gate to see two galloping riders coming toward the fort. Seeing the riders, he ordered the gate opened. He recognized Jonah from Harrison's main camp a month or so back. They had dined together at the officer's mess. Once inside the fort, Shipp greeted the two. He could tell by Jonah's look something was amiss.

"The British and Indians are out," Jonah volunteered after taking a breath.

"How big a force?"

Jonah turned to see a major standing there. Lieutenant Shipp quickly introduced the men. "Major, this is Jonah Lee from Washington. Mr. Lee, may I introduce you to our commanding officer, Major George Croghan."

As the two men shook hands, Croghan asked again, "Any estimate on the size of the force?"

"A quick estimate by a scout was five thousand or more, Major. It appeared they were headed to attack Fort Meigs. I was riding with a scouting party when we got the news. We were suddenly attacked by a large band of Indians. Captain Clay Gesslin and his group of Kentucky volunteers were trying to hold off the red devils long enough to give me a chance to get clear and warn you. Hopefully, some will survive and make it safely here."

"I see," Croghan replied. Another officer walked up and the major introduced him, "This is Captain Hunter, who is my second in command." Greetings were made and then Croghan continued, "We have a good position here. I think we can defend it against anything other than heavy artillery."

"If we had anything larger than the one six-pounder we could fire on any vessel attempting to pass the fort on the Sandusky," Hunter volunteered.

After looking around until he saw the stable, Moses took the reins of Jonah's horse and walked off to care for the animals.

"Your servant?" Croghan asked.

"My friend," Jonah replied quickly.

"I see," the major said, lowering his eyes and kicking the dirt.

"How many men do you have?" Jonah asked. "What's your strength?"

"One hundred and sixty," Croghan said, knowing it didn't sound like a lot. "We have three strong block houses with a sixteen foot high palisade stretching between the block houses. I've had a ditch dug around the palisade that's a good eight feet wide and just as deep. As I said, I believe we have a very defensible position. One I'd not like for the British to capture. They would then have a stronghold that would do as much damage to the war as Hull's surrendering Detroit."

Jonah liked Croghan and his officers. Croghan showed a degree of insight rarely found in someone so young. Sizing up the major, Jonah doubted Croghan was more than twenty or twenty-one years old.

"Indians!" The cry from the sentry had everyone climbing up to the parapet. The men watched as a number of braves wearing war paint passed by the fort on horseback. They were just outside of firing range.

Fresh scalps hung from their lances, and some of the braves shook them at the fort as they passed, taunting the men inside the fort.

"We can reach them with the six-pounder," Captain Hunter volunteered.

"No… I don't think so," Croghan said. "We have limited powder and shot for it. I'd prefer to put it to better use when the time arises."

That afternoon the sky turned dark and gray. Soon the distant roll of thunder was heard. Within an hour, they had a full blown thunderstorm. The rain was pouring down and bolts of lightning lit up the afternoon sky. It was under cover of the thunderstorm when more riders showed up. Gesslin and four of the ten men in the scouting party rode through the gates drenched and chilled. Gesslin had a bloody dressing around his arm. Not a single one of his men had escaped without some sort of wound.

"We held them off till it got dark," Gesslin said. "Then somehow we got separated. The other six may be alive, I don't know. A couple of men were badly wounded, but they may have made it."

The men were taken inside where their wet clothes were removed. While their clothes were being dried over a wood-burning stove, their wounds were treated. A hot meal was served which improved the men's spirits. Still wrapped in blankets, the men ate heartily. Jonah noticed a dollop or two of brandy had been added to the men's coffee. *They deserve it*, he thought.

"I'm grateful the Lawd seen fit to let 'em get through," Moses said. He'd come to like Gesslin and knew the man had put his life on the line along with those of the men in patrol so the fort could be warned. "It's possible some of those scalps the Indians carried may have been taken from Captain Clay's men," Moses whispered to Jonah.

"I've been thinking the same thing," Jonah replied. "But it won't do any good bringing up the possibility around Clay," he added.

"No, it won't," Moses agreed. "But I ain't forgetting about it."

"No… me neither," Jonah answered.

The rain was gone the next morning when Gesslin got up. Dressing quickly, he made it to the dining area in time for breakfast. His arm appeared stiff but he seemed to have full use of it otherwise. It didn't affect his appetite. At noon a cry rang out by the sentry of riders approaching.

Gesslin, Jonah, and Moses joined Major Croghan and Captain Hunter at the gate as three men rode into the fort. Their horses were wet and lathered from a long, hard ride.

"It's the British," the haggard scout blurted. "On land and on the river. It seems they are headed this way."

"What's their strength?" Major Croghan asked.

"I don't rightly know," the scout answered truthfully. "They's several gunboats, and I'd say at least five thousand injuns and soldiers combined."

Except for the addition of the gunboats, the estimated strength of the British hadn't changed since Jonah had arrived.

"Thank you," Croghan told the scout. "I'll have the sergeant fix you up with some grub."

"Sir, can we get some fresh horses?" the scout asked. "Ours are about played out. We've pushed them hard for a good twenty miles. We've had to outrun some of the red devils at times. They'll be hard put to make it back to General Harrison, played out as they be."

"I'm sure we can accommodate you," Major Croghan answered.

The scout look puzzled. "Do that mean yes?"

The officers all chuckled.

"Yes, that means yes," Croghan replied.

Now the scout grinned. "I'll be thanking you then, Major."

Croghan then spoke to the fort's officers, Gesslin and Jonah. "Let's meet in my office for a quick officer's call."

Cigars and pipes were lit up, and a glass of brandy was poured for each of the men. Once the glasses were filled, Major Croghan leaned back in his chair lighting his pipe. Soon, a small cloud of aromatic smoke drifted up. Satisfied the pipe was lit, the major took a swallow of his brandy then spoke.

"Well, it seems the odds have changed. I think we can stand an assault by ground troops and Indians. However, I'm not sure the fort can withstand a barrage of artillery. It may be best if we abandon the fort as General Harrison has recommended."

When none of the other men spoke, Jonah drained his glass of brandy and stood up. Taking a deep puff on his pipe, he blew out a cloud of smoke. "I disagree... respectfully," he added, giving a small salute with his pipe.

Leaning the chair forward so that all four legs touched the floor, Major Croghan said, "Oh."

"We talked about the tactical importance of the fort the day I arrived," Jonah said. "Nothing has changed to alter that. It may be the attack on Fort Meigs was just a feint to draw strength away from here. If that's so, the ploy has failed and we still have our full strength. We can fortify ourselves and make taking the fort a costly endeavor. We can also send out a volunteer asking for reinforcements. Even if we are overrun, we will have bought time for General Harrison to counter the British efforts."

Major Croghan nodded but didn't speak for a moment or so. "I agree," he finally said. "Any other thoughts?" Nobody spoke. "Well, I guess it's decided then. I'll prepare a quick dispatch stating our position and requesting reinforcements so the scout can take it with him when he leaves."

"Another glass," Croghan called to his servant and then sent for writing paper, quill, and ink. The dispatch was short.

"The fort is to be attacked by a superior force of British gunboats, soldiers, and Indian allies. Estimated number is five thousand or more. We

will not surrender. Reinforcements are requested." It was signed, Major George Croghan, U.S. Army, Commanding.

Chapter Six

ONCE AGAIN, THE SENTRY set off a cry of alarm. This had been occurring most of the day. The woods had been swarming with Indians since first light. At different times a group of young braves would make a dash toward the fort then stop just shy of musket range and taunt the defenders inside the walls. The officers had run to the parapet so many times it was getting hard to move with any urgency. This time, the cry that went up was different. There was a tremor to the sentry's alarm.

Jonah and Moses climbed the ladder to the parapet as two gunboats appeared at a bend in the river then continued toward a small cove just down from the fort. A small island in the stream would give some cover, so once the gunboats made it to the cove they could no longer be fired upon.

Major Croghan ordered the six pounder manned. Captain Hunter put his gunners to work and set up an immediate bombardment on the boats. The gunners worked feverishly to keep up a steady rate of fire. Hunter grew hoarse shouting, "Load, aim, fire, sponge out... sponge out, damn you... do you want the effen thing to explode in your face?"

Men ran to and from the magazine as quickly as they could carrying powder and shot. The gunboats were soon past the range and line of fire for the cannons. A few hits had been made with the men cheering every time they scored a hit. However, not one of the gunboats had been sunk or damaged so badly it didn't continue on. While the six-pounder was being fired, Indians revealed themselves in the woods from all directions. The fort was now surrounded, there would be no retreat.

Using his spy glass, Major Croghan called to Gesslin and Jonah. "Look there," he pointed toward the road with the barrel of his glass. Gesslin and Jonah took out their glasses, and when Captain Hunter walked up, Croghan handed him his glass. "That's Tecumseh in the lead," Croghan advised. The Indian chief with about two thousand braves was headed down the road away from the fort.

"They intend to cut off any reinforcement," Jonah stated.

Major Croghan nodded, "My thoughts as well. Not that I was expecting any."

"Sir, look there," Lieutenant Shipp volunteered. Three British officers under a flag of truce were heading toward the gates of the fort.

"Coming to offer an instrument of surrender," Jonah guessed.

"Have we had any second thoughts, gentlemen?" The major asked. When no one responded, he turned to Lieutenant Shipp, "Lieutenant, be so good as to meet our foe. Speak to them as gentlemen but tell them where to stick their terms of surrender."

The officers met just outside the gate. The junior British officer made the introductions. "Good afternoon to you, sir. I'm Captain Chambers of his Majesty's forty-first regiment. Colonel Elliott is our commanding officer and this chap is Captain Dixon, of the Royal Engineers. He is in command of our Indian allies."

Lieutenant Shipp, being as civil as he could be, shook each of the officer's hands and introduced himself.

After the greetings were completed, Colonel Elliott cleared his throat and spoke, as if reading from a prepared text. "*I am instructed to demand instant surrender of the fort, to spare the effusion of blood, which we can not do should we be under the necessity of reducing it by our powerful force of regulars, Indians, and artillery.*"

Lieutenant Shipp listened quietly to the long winded speech by the colonel. When the man had finished, Shipp paused only a second as he had already been forming his reply. "My commandant and the garrison," he replied, "are determined to defend the post to the last extremity and bury themselves in its ruins, rather than surrender it to any force what-so-ever."

Not believing his ears, Dixon spoke out, "But, sir, look at our immense body of Indians. They cannot be restrained from massacring the whole garrison, in the event of our undoubted success."

"And, sir, our success is certain," Captain Chambers eagerly added.

Shipp just looked at the men. Dixon, he felt, was truly concerned about controlling his "Indian allies." Feeling there was no more to say, Shipp turned to walk away when Dixon spoke again.

His voice beseeching, "It is a great pity that so fine a young man as you and as your commander is represented to be should fall into the hands of savages. Sir, for God's sake, surrender and prevent the dreadful massacre that will be caused by your resistance."

Shipp took a breath and responded coolly, "When the fort shall be taken, there will be none to massacre. It will not be given up while a man is able to resist." He then turned and headed back toward the fort.

As he passed a bushy ravine, an Indian jumped out attacking him. The Indian tried to snatch his sword away from him. Shipp pulled his pistol and was about to dispatch the savage when Captain Dixon called the brave off. Standing, with one hand on his sword and pistol in his other hand, Shipp looked at the Indian with hatred in his eyes. Jonah had been standing next to Gesslin and Moses. Seeing the confrontation Moses had picked up his long rifle ready to assist the lieutenant if need be. Croghan had been standing on the rampart during the entire time, as well. Seeing Dixon intervene with the brave, Moses lowered his long rifle.

Croghan then called down to his lieutenant, *"Shipp, come in and we will blow them all to hell."*

Once he entered the fort, Shipp spoke to Moses, "I'm obliged. I saw you were ready to dispatch that savage."

"Wasn't nothing, sir, but the Indian was as close as he'll ever come to dying without actually being dead. Besides my Betsy, I 'spect that brave had enough muskets trained on his body he'd been cut to doll rags had he hurt you."

"Well, thank you anyway," Shipp said.

The British officers had barely returned to their post when the air seemed to explode. Shells exploded all about creating craters where they hit the ground causing it to tremble.

"Damn," Jonah cursed. "Why'd you make them so mad, Major?"

Croghan smiled momentarily. "That's not regular field artillery."

"I agree," Jonah responded. "They must have landed one of those howitzers and set it up while the colonel was demanding surrender."

The whine of another shell was heard followed by an explosion.

"That's got to be one of the five and a half inch guns," Hunter volunteered, jerking as another shell landed. "Major, they seem to be concentrating most of their fire in this area. I think they noted the location from which the six-pounder was fired. I believe they're after the cannon, only they haven't zeroed in on it yet."

"I believe you are right. I'll have the sergeant shift it around. Maybe it will confuse them. Possibly even make them think we have several cannons instead of just the one."

The cannon was shifted from one position to another, keeping up a steady barrage. This was done until a sweaty powder-stained soldier ran up to Croghan. The man gave a haphazard salute then reported. "Major Croghan, the sergeant said I should tell you we getting mighty low on powder and shot."

Turning to Hunter, Croghan said, "Captain, have the men cease firing."

The sun had gone down, and it had gotten dark. The only thing the men had to fire at now was flashes. The British had unloaded more guns from the gunboats and continued firing. Lieutenant Shipp had been standing on the rampart. Seeing Jonah and Moses approach, he walked over to where they came up the ladder. "I count at least five six-pounders in addition to the howitzer," he volunteered. "You can tell the difference when they fire the howitzer compared to the six-pounders." It appeared the young lieutenant had made a quick study of the British guns. "The big howitzer will fire, and then each of the six-pounders will follow in succession." *He's had plenty of time to study the guns*, Jonah thought.

The British started firing somewhere about five p.m. and had not let up. It was now almost seven p.m. and dark. Undoubtedly, they had no shortage of powder and ball.

"They don't appear to be very good marksman," Shipp stated. "You'd think by now we'd have gaping holes in the wall."

"It's too dark to do anything other than harass us," Jonah answered. "I'm not an artillery man, but I wonder if the range might not be a bit much. They'll likely try to get a couple of guns closer in under the cover of darkness."

Taking a deep breath, Shipp said, "It was all a bunch of words about fighting to the last man today, but now, once the talking is over and the big guns are blazing away, I've realized we may actually have to die... here... fighting behind these walls." After a pause, he asked, "Do you ever get scared, Jonah?"

"Lots of times; not right now though... but tomorrow. The British will throw all they have at us. So far, it's just been a bunch of noise, but tomorrow when you can see them coming. That's when you'll get scared."

Hearing footsteps, the men turned to see a sergeant. "Sir," the sergeant said, speaking to Shipp. "The major said to get a detail of men and meet Captain Hunter at the middle block-house."

That was on the north side, Jonah recalled. He had walked the area with Croghan and Hunter that afternoon. They had walked all the way around the fort, and that was where Croghan felt the main attack would come from.

"There would be a rush toward all sides, but this was where the main force will attack," Croghan had said confidently.

Jonah had agreed with the major. Did he feel as sure now? Too late to second guess. You planned as best you could and adjusted accordingly. Jonah and Moses walked around the perimeter of the fort for something to do. At present they were mere spectators. Men were filling flour sacks to be used to reinforce any breaks in the palisade walls if that should happen.

"Think we should lend a hand?" Jonah asked.

"Wouldn't hurt any," Moses replied. "Besides, a little exercise will help you rest better."

"Think we'll be busy tomorrow?" Jonah asked his friend.

"Like as not, but you never know what the Lord has got planned."

"Well, hopefully, he'll be on our side tomorrow," Jonah said picking up a shovel.

Moses picked up a flour bag so Jonah could fill it with dirt and said, "Tomorrow! I pray he's on our side everyday."

Chapter Seven

JONAH WOKE UP AT dawn. Moses was already up and about. As Jonah washed up and then dressed, he realized the cannon fire was still roaring. He felt it was amazing that he could sleep through the barrage. The British must not have let up all night. He had not been awakened, so thus far there was little urgency among the fort's defenders.

The door to the room he'd been sleeping in opened and Moses came in. The two men had been together so long that when Jonah looked to Moses as if to say, *are we in danger*, Moses just shook his head. No words had passed.

After putting on his boots, Jonah asked, "Have you eaten?"

"No," Moses answered. "It'll be a slim breakfast, fatback and bread. All this cannon fire has scared the chickens, so they won't lay."

"There's coffee?" Jonah asked.

"Plenty," Moses replied. "Hot and black."

"Well, I've got by on less."

"That's the truth," Moses said in agreement.

As the two men walked across the edge of the parade ground to the kitchen, a roar and a crash was heard. Running toward the area where the crash had come from, they could see a part of the palisade had taken a hit, and a section about four feet wide and two feet high was stove in.

Captain Hunter was already directing men to pile bags of sand against the area to fortify and reinforce it. Seeing Jonah, Hunter walked over. "Sleep well?" he asked with a smile.

"It was like they were playing a lullaby," Jonah replied.

"Well, it might get worse this morning," Hunter volunteered. "They moved up their cannons during the night. They're up on a rise at the edge of the woods. At first we thought they'd just slowed down their rate of fire, then an hour or so ago we saw the flashes when they fired, so it was obvious they had been moved."

"Hoping for greater range by moving to higher ground," Jonah thought aloud. "Has it helped?"

Hunter used his thumb to point over his shoulder to the damaged palisade. "Some but not much," he said.

"Have we lost anyone yet?" Jonah asked.

"No... nothing more than a few with splinters so far."

"Thank the Lord," Moses interjected.

Major Croghan walked up. "I'm on my way to the officer's mess," he said, ignoring the cannon's fire. "Have you men broke your fast?"

When they stated they hadn't, Croghan said, "Well, join me. We may not have time for a leisurely lunch." This brought a chuckle from the group. Jonah motioned for Moses to come along with the group.

As they headed to the officer's mess, Hunter called to Sergeant Benson, "Send for me if need be."

"Yes sir," the sergeant replied.

"Sounds like a Kentuckian," Jonah volunteered.

"Most of us are," Croghan answered. "Doubt they could win this war without us."

"Well, I won't disagree since you're buying breakfast," Jonah joked but realized the major's words were probably far truer than he realized. It appeared most of the men he'd met were either Kentucky or Ohio volunteers.

Entering the officer's mess, Jonah was glad to see Clay Gesslin was already there sipping on a cup of coffee. As the officers sat down, Gesslin raised his cup in salute.

"I was beginning to think it was a holiday and you were sleeping in." Moses laughed at Gesslin's comments.

"Mosley," Croghan called to the cook. "What have you got for us this morning?"

"Fatback, biscuits and oatmeal."

"Is there any sugar?" Croghan asked.

"If the captain hasn't taken it like he did the flour, we do."

Croghan turned his head toward Hunter for an explanation.

"I'm about out of sandbags," Hunter said. "So I had a couple carts loaded with the sacks of flour and rice, ready to be used if needed."

"Good thinking, Captain. I hope you left a few in reserves in case we get hungry."

When Hunter didn't reply, Croghan sighed and said, "Well, eat hearty, men. Our menu may be limited later." They all laughed, but the reality was that there may not be a need for the supplies and each of the men knew it.

After finishing their breakfast, the men lingered over a last cup of coffee. The incessant roar of the cannons continued without respite. To break the monotony, Jonah asked, "How did Fort Stephenson come to be?"

Croghan replied, "This used to be a Catholic mission and a trading post. Located right on the river as it was, General Harrison was quick to see the strategic importance of it. The general had already started on Fort Meigs. Once it was completed, we built Fort Stephenson. Later, Fort Ball was built. General Harrison felt they would help protect the navigable waterways. By that, he was referring to the Maumee and Sandusky Rivers and the trail to the Scioto River. That's called the Sandusky – Scioto Trail for obvious reasons." Croghan continued. "Harrison felt protecting this was critical so that it could be used for our army in trying to defend the northwest portion of Ohio."

Jonah was not surprised to hear that Harrison's hand was in the planning. He'd always been a good strategist. "There aren't any other trails?" Jonah asked.

"Not many," Croghan acknowledged. "The rest of the land for the most part is swampy and so heavily wooded, traveling through it is almost impossible."

"We got a taste of that didn't we, Clay?" Jonah said recalling their travel to meet up with the army in Franklinton.

Croghan took a sip of coffee then continued his narrative of the fort's origin. "The construction of the fort was done in 1812. When I took command in 1813, I could see the fort would never stand an attack of any size. We erected two more block-houses and built an embankment and dug the ditch. Anyone trying to assault the fort will find it hard going and at a heavy price."

"I just hope General Proctor sees the difficulty," Jonah said.

"I think he has, otherwise, why the twelve hours of bombardment?" Lieutenant Shipp volunteered.

"You'd think," Gesslin interjected, "they would have heard it all the way to Washington and surely to Fort Meigs."

"Yes, well, with Tecumseh and a few thousand warriors between us and Fort Meigs, there's little General Clay can do," Croghan answered.

No sooner had Croghan finished speaking than a soldier knocked on the mess hall door and entered. Saluting, he spoke, "Sergeant Benson said you're needed, sir."

No one was sure who the man was addressing, probably Captain Hunter, but they all got up and followed the man to the wall and climbed the ladder to the rampart. The British appeared to have moved more of their guns, and now they opened up with a brisk rate of fire.

"You'd think those guns would get too hot to work," Lieutenant Shipp offered.

Watching the fall of the ball, Jonah wondered if the cannons' barrels had gotten too hot to give an accurate shot. "I guess the Lord is on our side today," he stated to Moses.

"Yes, but like I said, we need him with us today and everyday." Jonah smiled. He didn't disagree with Moses.

As the day progressed, breaks in the wall became far more numerous. Captain Hunter was now using the sacks of flour to shore up the wall. Seeing Jonah's gaze, Hunter shrugged at the man. By five o'clock, the bellowing of a distant thunderstorm on the western horizon was heard above the cannons. The rumbling continued and dark storm clouds were building. Was this an ominous sign?

"Here they come," someone shouted from the wall.

It appeared that with the foreboding thunderstorm, General Proctor's patience had run out.

For what we are about to receive, let us be grateful, Jonah thought as Moses ran for their weapons.

Chapter Eight

THEY ARE ATTACKING FROM the northwest and south," Croghan shouted as he approached his officers after making a hurried reconnoiter of the fort's walls. "Captain Hunter, take fifty men and go to the southern wall. Keep down until the redcoats are out of the woods in plain sight, and then give 'em hell. I will stay here, as I'm convinced this will be their main point of attack."

As Hunter turned to do as bid, Croghan placed his hand on the man's shoulder and called him by name. "James, keep your head down." The two men shook hands then Hunter rushed off. Suddenly, the ground shook and the roar of the enemy's guns was deafening.

"They've fired all their guns at once," Gesslin volunteered.

Within a minute, another round was fired. Balls crashed into the palisade wall, the block-house, and some even landed on the parade ground. Surprisingly, Jonah didn't see any casualties but the smoke from the cannons and howitzers was being carried toward them by the wind. Several men were already wiping their eyes, while others coughed from the smoke and the acrid smell of burnt gunpowder. Behind the smoke, the British made their move.

Seeing the distant advance, Croghan called to Sergeant Benson, "Who's your best gunner?"

"That would be Private Brown with the Petersburg volunteers, Major."

"Very well then, Sergeant. Since Private Brown is so skilled in gunnery, put him and his fellows in charge of the six-pounder."

"Will do, Major."

Within a few minutes, Private Brown was at Croghan's side. A quick salute was given and the private said, "Major, I need a good supply of rifle balls."

"Rifle balls?" Croghan asked, dismayed at the private's request.

"Yes sir. If we are to fire on troops, they will be a lot better than the six-pound balls. It will be like the navy firing canister or grape."

As Croghan hesitated, the private spoke again in a hurried voice. "Sir, it will be more like a shotgun than a musket."

Understanding, Croghan said, "Get what you need from the magazine."

Brown rushed off as the British guns fired again. The smoke was now so dense the fort's defenders hunkered down on the ramparts to seek some protection for their eyes.

It was Moses, with a wet rag tied over his nose and hat pulled low, who peeked over the wall and bellowed, "It's the British. They are on us." Looking at his friend, Moses held out his hand. Jonah grasped it firmly. No words were spoken, none were needed.

The British had made it to within twenty paces of the fort before they were noticed. They were in two columns, each led by a British officer.

"I don't see any Indians," Jonah said.

"Probably attacking the other wall," Croghan coughed his reply. As the British grenadiers closed to fifteen paces, he ordered, "Open fire."

Every man inside the fort had been at his post. Their guns were primed and loaded. Each of these Kentuckians was known as sharp-shooters. When the order to fire came, they rose from their cover and poured an intense shower of balls with such fatal precision that the British line broke as it was thrown into a mad confusion. While reloading his long rifle, Jonah could hear the British officers snapping orders and encouragement. The retreat faltered then the soldiers rallied. On the other side of the fort the sound of a pitched battle was heard. The sound of men shouting and cursing rose above the din of battle.

Hopefully, Captain Hunter and his men would be able to keep the British at bay. So far only the northwestern corner and the southern walls were being attacked. Croghan had put sixteen men on the eastern and western walls should they be attacked. That few men would not be able to hold off any sizable force, but they could hold off the enemy until reinforcements could be sent to help out.

The British now had axe-men working on the stakes driven into the ground of the embankment. It was hard not to admire the bravery of the soldiers as they hacked a path through the obstacles and under the constant fire of the fort's defenders.

One of the British officers, a colonel, was at the head of his gallant party. "Cut away the pickets, my brave lads," he yelled. "Show the damned Yankees no quarter."

The men now had a path opened up and they jumped into the ditch, which was muddy after the recent storms. They only had to make it up the steep side of the ditch to be at the fort's wall. *That would still be difficult*, Jonah realized, as in their haste the British had not thought to bring scaling ladders. As the number of British making their way into the ditch increased, Jonah wondered how much longer they would be able to hold off the British assault.

In the block-house, Brown and his men had loaded the six-pounder with rifle balls. He depressed the barrel so that it could fire into the ditch. He then ordered the cannons port to be opened and fired. The gun spoke with a devastating effect. Slugs and rifle balls poured into the attackers like a swarm of deadly bees. The destructive havoc was instantly recognized, but the British mounted a second assault.

Wiping the grime and smoke from his face, Gesslin shouted to be heard. "They don't know the word quit, do they?"

The riflemen kept up their rapid fire with such accuracy that redcoats fell in increasing numbers. How long would it be before the adrenaline gave out and the defenders would be too tired to continue? The second column of the storming party met with another volley from the six-pounder. The aftermath of the deadly discharge was sickening as Jonah peered down. The entire second column was down; most appeared dead including the two officers. *Could the British commander not see the carnage,* Jonah wondered.

Several from the forty-first regiment were climbing up the embankment in retreat. Some of the fort's sharpshooters continued to fire until Major Croghan roared out the order to cease fire. Jonah couldn't count the bodies as dead lay on top of fallen comrades. At least twenty-five had fallen with the last blast by the six-pounder.

The din of battle still filled the air on the other side of the fort, so Croghan dispatched another fifty men to assist those men. With the reinforcement, the British were assailed with such an onslaught of hot lead that the British officer broke off the attack and the redcoats fled for the protective shelter of the woods.

"It's over," Moses said as he handed a canteen to Jonah, who took a deep pull of the warm water. His mouth was dry and he had not realized how thirsty he had gotten.

"Lieutenant Shipp," Croghan called.

"Yes sir."

"Secure the men from their post except for a few sentries then assemble the men. Let me know what the cost has been."

Jonah knew the major was asking how many had been killed. It seemed like the attack had gone on forever but seeing the sun starting to set, Jonah looked at his watch and was amazed. The battle had only lasted about thirty minutes, though it seemed much longer.

Lieutenant Shipp returned in a few minutes and reported, "One dead, Major, and seven with minor wounds."

"Thank God," Croghan answered. "We have repulsed a major assault from two quarters with only one man dead and a few wounded."

"It was the last blast of the six-pounder that ended the contest," Shipp said. "That took the life out of them."

"I wonder where the Indians were," Gesslin said.

"The red devils apparently deserted the British. Had they participated the outcome may have been different."

"Possibly," Croghan admitted. "But I think not."

The dark storm clouds in the west passed northward as the rays from the setting sun beamed down.

"What splendor," Moses said, more articulate than usual.

A gentle breeze from the southwest swept the lingering fog of battle smoke away toward the forest.

"It's the Sabbath," Moses said.

"That's true," Croghan said.

As the twilight came, the major addressed his gallant little band with eloquent words of praise; he then said a prayer of grateful thanksgiving. Beyond the walls, the groans of the wounded British could be heard.

"We were truly blessed," Moses said as he made his way to the rampart.

"What are you going to do?" Jonah asked.

"See if I can help the wounded," Moses replied. Filling a bucket of water from a fire barrel, he tied a rope around the handle and lowered it over the wall.

Darkness fell and during the night many of the British dead were removed. All during the following morning, the wounded British were brought into the fort's small hospital and their wounds tended as best the small medical staff could. By noon, scouts were sent out and they soon returned stating the British had pulled out leaving one of the gunboats loaded down with military supplies. These were brought into the fort.

Jonah then approached Croghan and advised him that he and Gesslin were going to head back to General Harrison's camp. Croghan wrote a hurried report to the general and then thanked the men for their efforts.

"Hopefully we'll see each other soon," Croghan said as he shook each of the men's hands.

"Hopefully it will be under more pleasant circumstances," Jonah said.

This brought a smile from Croghan. "Hopefully," he said. "... hopefully."

Chapter Nine

A DEFINITE CHILL WAS IN the air as dawn made its way over the thick forest, and the sky changed from dark to a hazy gray. The bright yellow, brown and red leaves that held to the limbs of the hardwood trees were still black as the sun hadn't risen to the point the individual colors were distinguishable.

The sentry guarding the main entrance to Camp Seneca had his cloak pulled close about him. Gloved hands were still cold, made even more so by the chill of the steel musket barrel gripped so firmly in his hands. His nose was red and raw where a sleeve was used to wipe away the constant drip from a runny nose. Little clouds were created each time the man exhaled. The sentry was miserable... miserable and dangerous. It would not do for some sergeant to try to sneak up on him as he'd likely get a lead ball in his gut for breakfast. It would have been nice if the sentry had been allowed a fire, but this was denied by the general as it would point out the sentry's location.

However, any Indian who had made twelve summers would have had no problem locating the sentry. With all the stomping around, rubbing and clapping hands together to keep warm, the sentry may just as well have lit a fire. The only reason he had not lost his hair was the Indians were meeting their general.

Tecumseh was arguing with British General Procter about his failure to bring the Americans to a battle. He knew if the British didn't stand and fight, the tribes in the Confederation would lose the protection for their lands, which the British had promised if they would become their allies. Sensing the need to push Proctor into making a stand, Tecumseh faced Proctor and tried to force him into action by shaming him. "We must compare our father's conduct to a fat animal that carries its tail upon its back; but when afraid, it drops it between its legs and runs off."

Once the conversation was complete, Tecumseh realized Proctor could not be pushed and would not do battle on anything but his own terms. Therefore, when the sergeant came around with a private to relieve the miserable half-frozen sentry, he was still alive. Not because of any alertness on his part but because of the lethargy of British General Proctor.

Jonah and his group made their way into camp as the sun made its way over the trees. The sentry recognizing the group motioned them forward without calling for the sergeant of the guard. After unsaddling their horses, Captain Clay Gesslin shook hands with Jonah and Moses, stating he'd look up Colonel Johnson and report in. Jonah was tempted to make his way to the officer's mess tent and break his fast but decided to report to General Harrison first. He was sure a hot cup of coffee would be offered. Moses took the bedrolls to their tent and made his way to the mess tent. The two would meet back at their campsite later.

Jonah was surprised to see twice the number of men gathered around General Harrison's tent. Something was in the making… and with all the different uniforms, it had to do with the Navy. Making his way into the general's crowded tent, Jonah thought he'd just listen without interrupting or getting involved.

However, Harrison's wandering eye spotted him and called out, "By all that's mighty, our Washington man is back and still has his hair."

This caused everyone to turn and greet Jonah. A few chuckled at the general's comments.

Harrison stood, shook Jonah's hand and said, "I'm glad you're back safe and sound. We'll talk about the battle at Fort Stephenson later, but now I want you to meet Commodore Oliver Hazard Perry."

Once the introductions were made, Harrison caused Jonah to flinch as he told Perry, "Mr. Lee is here on behalf of John Armstrong and President Madison to make sure we carry on this war in a manner suitable to the administration. By that, I mean we are to be both aggressive and economical."

Another round of chuckles filled the tent causing Jonah to flush once more. However, Harrison draped his arm across Jonah's shoulder and spoke to the commodore.

"In truth, Oliver, Jonah is a brave man. One I'd trust my life with. He's a fighter, not a bureaucrat. The commodore, Jonah, is here to do away with the British presence on the lakes. If we can do away with their ships, we limit the supplies being furnished to the army and several garrisons."

One of the general's aides then entered the tent, "Sir, breakfast is ready. Due to the number of guests, would you prefer it to be served in the officer's mess?"

After a quick glance around the tent, Harrison said, "Yes, I think that would be preferable."

As the officers made their way in to the officer's mess, Jonah found himself sitting across from Perry. Once breakfast was served the men ate heartily. Platters heaping with fried eggs, ham, sausage, and mounds of fried potatoes were placed in front of the hungry men. Hot bread was served with fresh preserves and blackberry jelly. The coffee was hot...hot, black, and strong.

After finishing his meal, Perry seemed ready to talk and found Jonah a ready listener. "The British have maintained control of Lake Erie for over a year," Perry began. "With this control they have been able to establish a supply route from Fort Malden to Port Dover. We have been able to raid the British outposts, but until now we've not had the ships and firepower to take on the British with any chance of winning. We are still outnumbered, and the British have just completed construction on a new flagship I'm told. I'm not sure how many guns she's to mount at this point, but I'm told they'll be long nines."

"Do we carry the same?" Jonah asked.

"No," Perry said, his voice excited. "We carry carronades. The carronades are shorter guns which carry a much heavier ball and can wreak much more havoc and destruction. They are affectionately called smashers by the gunners. The disadvantage is the range. The range of a long nine is a mile. The carronades effective range is half that. Therefore, to be effective we have to move in close. We have a few long guns but the smashers make up our main armament."

"Won't they be able to pick us apart at the greater distance?" Jonah asked.

Perry's reply was short and blunt. "Aye, they'll try."

Harrison then joined into the conversation and asked, "How do we compare in numbers, Oliver?"

The commodore paused and took a sip of coffee. "At last report, the British squadron is made of six ships armed with sixty-three cannons. This does not count the new *Detroit*."

"And our ships?" Harrison asked.

"We now have a flotilla comprised of nine vessels mounting fifty-four guns."

Jonah did not miss the use of vessels instead of ships when the commodore spoke. General Harrison either missed the difference or chose not to pursue it. Rather he asked, "What about our men, are they ready?"

"Aye, they are ready and eager. The days of gun and sail drill have honed these men into a fighting crew. The British, on the other hand, are not so well-manned. My spies tell me their ships are manned with a few seamen, but the majority of the crews are made up of poorly trained British soldiers, Canadian militia and provincial mariners. Therefore," the commodore said as he wiped his face with a handkerchief then pushed his chair back, "I believe we can put an end to the British control of the lake... God willing."

The men then focused their attention to breakfast and it was soon finished. Jonah rose as Harrison and Perry stood up. A few of the officers followed as the two men left the officer's mess. A servant refilled Jonah's coffee cup, and he sat back down. He was not a sailor but understood without the water supply route the British in the northwest could not survive. Therefore, it was imperative the commodore beat the British. Finishing his cup, Jonah made his way back to his tent to write his report on Fort Stephenson and the need to end British occupation of the Great Lakes. As he finished his report, he added, 'I feel Commodore Perry is a man of action and the right man to deal with the British on the lake. My question is, does he have the forces at his disposal to accomplish the task?'

Chapter Ten

THE NEXT FEW DAYS were lazy ones. The mornings and evenings were cool, but the temperatures climbed during the middle of the day. Moses complained about the fluctuations in temperature.

"Blast it all, I don't know if I'm going to burn up or freeze. A jacket is too much and a shirt ain't enough."

Jonah couldn't help but smile at his friend. It was not the temperatures bothering Moses but the boredom. Since returning from Fort Stephenson and meeting with Commodore Perry very little had transpired, but today was sure to be different.

Commodore Perry had sent word to General Harrison that his vessels were ready to take on the British fleet. For some time now Perry's little squadron had been blockading the water route between Long Point and Amherstburg, aggravating the shortages in the British camp. Spies had related the British were short on food, blankets, and medicine... everything but ammunition.

"That's no wonder," General Harrison boasted. "They haven't fired a shot since the attack on Fort Stephenson."

The spies also related that the carronades and other guns which had been ordered for the newly constructed Detroit had not arrived. Robert Herloft Barclay, the British Naval Commander, had shifted ordinance from Fort Malden to arm the ship. After a meeting between Barclay and General Proctor, the decision was to attack Commodore Perry's vessels and put an end to the blockading.

Commodore Perry sailed into Sandusky Bay amid a sky of heavy, dark clouds.

"It's going to rain for sure," Moses grumbled. "Hot, cold and now wet, I don't know what's worse, freezing, baking or drowning." Moses had voiced the same complaint many of the Kentucky volunteers had complained of.

"You've been around the Kentucky militia so much you sound like them," Jonah chided his friend.

"I'd hate to hear how bad you'd complain if you had the chilblain," Moses snorted then said, "It's where I was stuck by the Creek arrow that gets me into such a misery."

"Maybe it's the knowledge General Harrison has invited Chief Tarhe and his band of Wyandots into the camp that's got you shirred up," Jonah suggested.

"That don't help none," Moses agreed.

Jonah had mixed feelings about the peace overture to the Wyandots, but even if they couldn't count on the tribe as allies, if they'd remain neutral and not back the British that would in itself be a blessing.

"Mr. Lee."

"Yes," Jonah replied as he turned to find Lieutenant Walters, one of General Harrison's officers, speaking.

"The general's compliments, sir. Commodore Perry has sent boats to transport the general and members of his staff out to the... ah... flagship. The general felt you might enjoy the outing, sir."

Outing indeed, Jonah thought looking at the sky. He then turned toward Moses who made a backhanded waving motion.

"You go," he said. "I'm like Captain Clay's men. Given the choice I'll stick to horses and dry land."

Jonah shook his head and asked, "When do we depart, Lieutenant?"

"The boats are waiting now, sir."

"Yes, I imagine they are," Jonah replied. "Let me get my raincoat, and we'll be on our way."

Moses had rustled up a cup of coffee by the time Jonah was leaving. Ducking under a tent flap as the first drops of rain started to fall, Moses smiled and said, "Keep dry."

By the time Jonah had arrived at Harrison's tent, he found the general had offered to take the Indians aboard Commodore Perry's ship to see firsthand the power the Americans were ready to unleash on the British.

Not one to speak profanity, Jonah hissed, "What a shitten mess this is gonna be."

"I agree, sir," Lieutenant Walters replied.

Not realizing he'd spoken aloud, Jonah flushed. However, it was satisfying to know he was not the only one with the same opinion.

By the time the boats were rowed out to the *Lawrence*, Jonah was soaked through and through. What little water had not found its way down the neck of the coat had been sloshed over the sides of boats, so he was wet from one end to the other. Unfamiliar with the navy tradition of firing salutes, Jonah almost jumped over the side when the cannons went off saluting General Harrison.

"Damn," he shouted.

"Easy sir," one of the sailors consoled him. "It was just a salute for the general."

"Well, you might have warned me before hand."

Even though the sailor seemed sincere, Jonah didn't miss the snickers behind him. *I wonder how the Wyandots reacted*, he thought to himself. He didn't really care if the heathens had been warned before time. Serve the sailors right if a few heads had been bashed after the cannon fired its salute, however. Jonah's boat hooked onto the *Lawrence* just in time for him to watch the Indians swarm over the sides of Perry's ship. As the Indians poked about the ship, Jonah grasped a firm grip on the hand ropes and made his way up the slippery battens. *Well, at least I didn't wind up with a dunkin in Lake Erie*, he thought as he made his way through the entry port.

There, he was met by one of the commodore's lieutenants. Not sure about naval protocol, Jonah gave a salute, doffed his hat and reached out to shake the lieutenant's hand. Watching the lieutenant's face, it was easy for Jonah to realize he'd confused the officer. However, there was a smile on the lieutenant's face when he took Jonah's offered hand.

It was apparent he knew who Jonah was as he said, "I'm Lieutenant Jones, Mr. Lee. The commodore and the general have already gone below so if you'll follow me we will join them."

The lieutenant either omitted or forgot to tell Jonah to lean over. No sooner had he made his way down the small companion ladder and entered the commodore's cabin than he butted his head on a beam. He staggered as stars flashed before his eyes.

"Damn it, man," Commodore Perry hissed at Jones. "Did you neglect to warn our guest to duck?"

Lieutenant Jones looked contrite and worried so that Jonah felt it had not been a purposeful omission. God help the sod if he ever found out different, though.

As soon as Jonah was able to fully get his wits about him, he found he was having his knot examined by both the commodore and the general.

"It'll likely swell as big as a goose egg but shouldn't bleed," the commodore stated.

"It's how much it rattled my brain I'm worried about," Jonah managed to say.

"No worries there," General Harrison replied, trying to be humorous. The only response he got for his efforts was a glare from Jonah.

Commodore Perry offered a glass of wine and again offered his apology for the accident. "A bad beginning, Mr. Lee, when I was planning on asking if you have the desire to spend a few days sailing with us."

Jonah was not sure how to answer. He had no desire to be a sailor but this might be an experience that might not arise again. It would certainly be something he could add in his report to the president, a view of the war from a different vantage point. "I'll consider it," Jonah finally answered.

"Our friend," General Harrison said to the commodore, "is much more at home astride a horse than trying to dodge beams aboard ship."

"Ahem... well, you have until the morrow to decide, Mr. Lee," the commodore stated.

At that time Lieutenant Jones returned. "The weather is deteriorating, sir, and the savages... ah, the Indians appear ready to leave the ship."

General Harrison went on deck and talked with Chief Tarhe again while Commodore Perry had a crew for the boats rousted out to row the Wyandots back to shore.

Once they had departed, General Harrison spoke to Jonah, "Do you feel the chief is a man of his word?"

Jonah hesitated a moment to collect his thoughts, then replied, "I do as long as you understand his word is just that... his word. If several of his braves decide not to follow it, they just split off and go their own way."

"As I thought," the general replied. "For whatever its worth, Chief Tarhe was mighty impressed with the ship's big guns. He has promised his tribe will not support the redcoats."

"Did he say they'd support us?" Jonah asked.

"No, he didn't go that far. While he's not for us, at least he's not against us."

"Aye, that's better than nothing." This was from the commodore who'd returned without the others hearing him. He then informed the two men, "My steward has informed me dinner is ready if we are."

Suddenly Jonah was starving. The mention of food reminded him he'd not eaten since early that morning. The aroma of beef had been in the air for a while, but it hadn't dawned on him what it was he'd smelled. *But how could* it, he thought to himself, *after being knocked senseless, it was a wonder I can do anything at all. Well, I'll sample the shipboard fare and if it beat camp cooking I'll spend a few days with the Navy.*

Chapter Eleven

THE FOLLOWING MORNING BROUGHT a clear sky but enough wind to cause the waters to have a significant chop to them. Jonah awoke but lay still in his cot trying to clear his mind from a fog. His unfamiliar surroundings didn't help. There was a rocking motion to his cot. He'd never slept in a cot suspended from deck beams by four ropes. It didn't seem right a man's bed should move like a baby's cradle. Ah... the taste in his mouth and his aching head. Was the pounding in his head from butting the deck beam or the effects of last evening's gathering?

It took a few more seconds for him to realize the sound in his head was not from butting his head nor the abundance of after dinner brandy along with cigar and pipe smoke. They didn't help, but after a few minutes he was able to recognize the constant thud was from the lap of the choppy water against the hull of the ship. As he rose, he looked over the small cabin... cubical was a better description. Looking for his clothes, he spotted them and was at the point of putting his boots on when a small knock was heard. A man wearing an apron stuck his head in the door.

"I see you're almost dressed," the man said. "There's a small pitcher of water and a basin in the corner. Once you've freshened yourself, the commodore and general are expecting you in the commodore's quarters."

Rushing to freshen up, Jonah made his way to the commodore's quarters. One look at Jonah and the commodore was quick to order a cup of coffee for him. Greeting the commodore and general, Jonah seated himself in the offered chair and took a timid sip of the hot, steamy black liquid.

"The navy likes their coffee so strong you can stand a spoon in the middle of the cup," General Harrison volunteered.

"I see, sir," Jonah acknowledged, tasting the scalding brew.

The coffee was strong, but after a couple of sips it started to bring him back to life. Maybe he would survive the day. Cordial conversation ensued until a breakfast of scrambled eggs, crisp bacon, oatmeal and hot bread with grape preserves was served. Jonah noticed during the meal the commodore's steward never let the coffee cups get half empty before they were refilled. He did notice while a dish of sugar was on the table, it had not been offered, and except for the oatmeal it had been left untouched. In the past, Jonah had been offered cream and sugar for his coffee. *I guess the navy likes it black and strong,* he thought, realizing it didn't take much to acquire a taste for the brew. No cream had been offered to mix with the oatmeal either. *Maybe they don't have any,* Jonah thought.

The commodore had mixed butter in his oatmeal along with the sugar. Jonah tried this and found it tasty. Still, a little milk would have added to the taste. Once breakfast was finished and the dishes cleared away... all but the coffee, General Harrison cleared his throat.

"Tell me, Jonah, do you think a few of the Kentucky riflemen would mind serving aboard the commodore's ships?"

Thinking again to Clay Gesslin's men's comments about fighting on boats compared to horses, he replied, "I'm not sure about the foot soldiers, but I don't think the mounted riflemen would take to it. May I ask why you ask, sir?"

Shaking his head in the affirmative, the general responded, "The Navy has enough vessels to take on the British. We also have more firepower, it is believed. What they don't have are the men to fight the ships. The commodore has asked for volunteers."

"How many?" Jonah asked.

"Two or three dozen," the commodore answered.

Taking it all in Jonah thought for a few moments, then replied, "If put to the men just right, you could get your men I expect."

"How do you mean 'put to them just right'?" the general asked, a hint of bitterness in his voice.

"You could just order them to serve," Jonah responded. "But remember these are volunteers. I would put it to them that the Navy needed their help. They'd have three square meals a day, and there'd be no slogging through the woods or boggy, muddy roads. The ships would carry them to the fight, and a glorious fight it will be. In fact, they'd be going in style. But you can only take three dozen, so the men would have to make a quick decision before someone else volunteered, as it would be first come, first serve."

The commodore reared back and clapped his hands. "You silver tongued devil. I like it. Sir, you could be a politician."

Smirking, General Harrison replied, "He works for one." Then the general smiled and pounded Jonah on the back. "No offense, Jonah. I don't know what we'd do without you."

The following morning three dozen Kentucky riflemen showed up. Having accepted the challenge or the lark, Jonah wasn't sure which; they climbed aboard the Lawrence and seemed as excited as Chief Tarhe's Wyandots had been. The commodore let them have the run of the deck for an hour then called them all forward. A lieutenant mustered them into ranks and instructed them in the ways of naval discipline and explained to them the etiquette of life aboard a ship at sea.

"I thought this here's a lake we's on," one of the men said.

The officer then explained that it was the same, the Great Lakes or the ocean, made no difference.

That evening Jonah dined alone with the commodore. "It will be soon," the commodore stated in a matter of fact voice, once the meal was served. He seemed in a different mood tonight. One like Jonah had not observed before. It was like he had an appointment with death and was resolved to it.

"Do you realize," the commodore spoke after a period of silence, "that the fate of this war... this country looms on our battle with the British? A battle where the loss of one vessel could mean the difference between victory or defeat."

The commodore then smiled. "Have you thought what it would be like to answer to the king again rather than have a president?"

"No sir," Jonah answered. "I don't think I've ever given it much thought."

"I have and it doesn't sit well," the commodore replied.

Jonah went to bed in his swinging cot that evening. For some reason, Moses came to his thoughts and he was glad he was ashore. Moses could take the word back to his family if he fell. The next morning, Jonah awoke at four a.m. As he made his way on deck, he met one of the ship's officers he'd come to be friendly with.

"Have you heard?" the officer whispered.

"What?" Jonah asked.

"The commodore... he's down with the fever. The surgeons are with him now."

Damn, Jonah thought. Maybe that's why he was in such a mood last evening. What bad timing. "Damn it all," he cursed again. What chance would they have without the commodore?

Jonah continued on deck where he met up with a sergeant from the Kentucky riflemen. He had a detail of men carrying buckets of water down to the galley.

"What are you doing?" Jonah asked.

"The surgeon's orders, sir. He thinks it's the lake's water what has caused the fever and dysentery. He's ordered all water used to drink or cook with be boiled beforehand."

"From what I 'ears not only is the commodore sick but so is his brother, most of the ossifers two of the surgeons and several men from the crew," the sergeant whispered.

"You appear well," Jonah said.

"We all is," the sergeant replied, speaking of the riflemen. "Course we drink our own drink."

By that Jonah knew the men drank either vinegar and water or corn whiskey and water, the water being the lesser ingredient. Jonah had learned riding with Clay Gesslin the only plain water the men drank was when it came from a well or fast moving stream. *I've not been sick either*, Jonah thought. But other than the coffee which had been boiled, he'd not drunk more than a swallow or two of ship's water in days. He'd been given a fresh canteen by Moses each time he'd gone ashore. Well, he'd go ashore today and get a couple more canteens of clean water... and maybe one of corn whiskey. He had little doubt Moses could round up one from the mounted riflemen.

It was five a.m., September tenth. Three days after the fever had spread among the officers and crew of the Lawrence. Jonah had been awake since four a.m., as had been happening of late. Unlike the card games and campfire gatherings he was used to with the army, the navy had set watches and when not on watch, the men rested. They gathered about on deck and in their messes below deck, but when lights out was called the ship became very quiet.

Jonah missed the whinny of the horses, the giggle of some wench the men had snuck into camp and hid in their tent, the crackle of the campfire and the fresh air. The smell aboard ship was insulting to the nostrils. Not that he didn't understand it; from all the unwashed bodies to the stale water in the bilges, there was no way a ship could be without odor. But it was a special place, and while Jonah would never be a sailor, he was glad for the experience.

"Sail ho, sails on the horizon." The cry from the mainmast of the *Lawrence* caused an immediate rush of activity aboard the ship. The commodore was on deck talking with the first officer. After giving the orders for the ships to weigh anchor and set sail, the commodore strode over to Jonah. *He still looks pale and weak*, Jonah thought. But there was fire in the commodore's eyes.

"We will meet the British today, Mr. Lee. I don't know if I told you but our foe, Commander Robert Barclay, is a most capable and experienced Royal Navy officer who fought with Lord Nelson at Trafalgar in 1805. I hear he lost an arm fighting the French a few years later. A most capable man, an honorable opponent," the commodore repeated.

The second cry of sail ho interrupted the commodore's conversation. "Where away," the commodore called up to the masthead lookout.

"To the northwest, sir," the reply came down. "Several ships sir, more like the whole British squadron.".

Taking his telescope and peering toward the oncoming British fleet, the commodore ordered the signal lieutenant to make, "Enemy in sight."

The ship's master made his way to where Jonah and the commodore were standing. "It appears they will have the weather gauge," he volunteered.

"I don't care," the commodore snapped. "To windward or leeward, we shall fight today."

Jonah had no idea what the two were talking about. Lieutenant Jones, seeing the quandary, explained having the wind at their advantage or having to fight the wind. The sun rose and the sky was clear but with light air. For two hours the commodore's vessels clawed to windward, repeatedly tacking in an effort to close with the British.

At ten-thirty a.m., Commodore Perry appeared very frustrated. "We'll not bring them to battle before noon," he said addressing his first lieutenant. "Have the men served their midday meal."

"Aye, aye," the lieutenant answered. As he turned to carry out the commodore's orders, Perry spoke again.

"Lieutenant."

"Yes sir."

"A double tot of grog for every man."

Hearing this, the crew gave a cheer. *Leave it to the commodore to fortify the men for battle*, the lieutenant thought.

Chapter Twelve

AFTER THE MIDDAY MEAL and grog had been served, Commodore Perry had the ship 'beat to quarters' and 'clear for action.' Jonah felt that he was in the way as he watched what looked like mass confusion quickly turn the ship into a battle ready state. He could hear the noise below the decks as partitions were struck down and stowed. He watched as the surgeon's mates ran about setting up the place where the wounded would be treated. The deck was doused with water and sand spread across them.

A harried petty officer quickly explained blood made the deck slippery. The wet sand would help with grip. Jonah had faced death in battle many times, but the callousness of the sailor's abrupt explanation made him shiver.

The wooden stoppers called tampions were removed from the mouth of the guns. Looking at the brutes, Jonah recalled the commodore saying they'd have to be close for the carronades to be effective. Did he think the British would wait until they got in range? *Much like the long rifle compared to the musket,* he thought. A few men with long rifles could standoff a company of infantry with muskets by picking them off before the infantry closed to within range.

Not far away, Jonah could hear a sailor explain to one of the Kentucky riflemen how the battle would likely proceed. "The commodore will try to get the weather gauge. That will give us-un's the chance to cross the British's ships and rake 'em. We'll have our guns blazin so that we blast them from stem to stern."

Seeing the frown on the Kaintuck's face with the use of stem to stern, the sailor quickly added, "That's from the front to the back. If it's done right, they'll not likely even get a shot at us. Course, sometimes they do, and then it's like the infernal pits 'o hell."

Taking a breath, the sailor looked about. Seeing he had an audience, he wiped his whiskery jaw then continued, "Now, more often than not, two ships will collide. When that happens, grappling hooks get throwed about so the ships get tied together. Iffen that happens, it's a free for all with the winner taking all... or what's left. There'll be marines and sailors swarming all about. Some will have swords or cutlasses and even some of them boarding pikes like I already showed you. Others will have pistols and tomahawks and such. People will be firing swivel guns, sharpshooters will bang away with rifles and officers will have pistols, like I said. You'll hear officers shouting orders, men screaming in pain, some cussing and some praying. You live through this, boy, you can say you're going to habben cause you done been to hell."

"Sir."

Jonah turned. He'd not heard the lieutenant approach.

"The commodore's compliments, sir. Would you join him in his cabin?"

"Thank you," Jonah replied and made his way aft.

Entering the commodore's cabin, Jonah found the man tearing up letters and throwing them out the stern windows. "Letters from my wife," Perry said, by way of explanation. "I'd not want the British to have them if I fell or was captured."

Throwing the last fragments out, the commodore then tied a set of official looking documents in a bundle with a small cannon ball. "These are to go over the side if we are taken," the commodore explained. "The first lieutenant has been instructed to deal with it if I'm unable. Should we both fall, I leave it in your care."

Realizing this was a sacred trust, Jonah felt moved. "They will not be taken as long as I breathe, sir."

"Good. Now, I called you down to offer you a brace of pistols and your choice of a cutlass or sword."

"I know nothing of either, sir. I have a sharp tinker-made knife and pistol. I also have my tomahawk. The other pistols will be appreciated, but I'll leave the long blades to someone else."

Back on deck, Jonah watched as the British and American ships sailed toward each other. Lieutenant James walked up to Jonah. "Makes a magnificent sight, don't it, sir? Two fleets preparing to do battle. We may never see such a sight again."

"Do we know the British ships we are fighting?" Jonah asked.

"Yes sir," James answered. "Commodore Barclay's fleet is made up of the *Detroit, Queen Charlotte, Lady Prevost,* the *Hunter,* the *Chippewa,* and the *Little Belt.*"

"And our ships are the *Lawrence, Niagara,* and the *Caledonia,*" Jonah said.

Lieutenant James replied, "Yes sir, those are three of our ships. We also have the *Ariel, Scorpion, Somers, Porcupine, Tigress,* and the *Trippe.*"

"So, we have the most ships," Jonah commented.

"Aye," James replied. "But they have the most guns."

The crew was silent as each man was deep in his own thoughts. *Would we defeat the British? Will I fall? Who will care for my family if I fall?* So many questions and no answers. The only thing for sure is a battle was about to take place.

Suddenly, a cheer went up as the commodore ordered his blue banner run up. The banner read 'Don't give up the ship'. The banner was the battle slogan Perry used to honor the dying words of Captain James Lawrence. The captain had been a close friend who had died in battle on the first of June. The commodore's ship had been named for the fallen Lawrence.

As the *Lawrence* sailed forward, Lieutenant James looked aft and hissed, "Damn Elliott."

Elliott had been commander of the Great Lakes squadron until Commodore Perry had arrived. Some thought Elliott had lost his command due to Perry's political involvement with the senior senator from Rhode Island. Elliott had acted appropriately thus far. He was in command of the brig *Niagara* of twenty-two guns, the *Lawrence's* sister ship.

Following Jones's eyes, Jonah could see the Niagara seemed to be lagging behind. As the distance between the two squadrons narrowed, Lieutenant Jones spoke again in a nervous, trembling voice.

"Are we to take on the entire British squadron alone?"

The schooners *Ariel* and *Scorpion* were some distance off the weather bow. Caledonia was a small brig of only three guns and was further behind than either of the schooners or *Niagara*. A boom was heard, and Jonah saw a huge splash as the shot fell short.

The commodore spoke to his first lieutenant, "Please note in the log, sir, at eleven forty-five, fired on by the British ship, *Detroit*."

Five minutes later a second shot was fired, only this time it was a hit. Jonah watched, as if in slow motion, the enemy ball smash into the side of the ship, the bulwarks exploding, sending wooden splinters high into the air. Two men were killed instantly; the ball turning their bodies into a bloody pulp.

The deck suddenly turned dark as the downed men's blood seeped out of their lifeless bodies mingling with the wet sand. Over the side, an officer barked. The mangled bodies were hastily scooped up by their mates and thrown over the side. A memorial service might be held later, but now they were in the way, with little enough left of either to recognize they'd once been men.

Commodore Perry ordered that the *Lawrence* be shifted in position so that they could return fire. By this time, cannon balls were raining down with cries of pain and anger all about. Petty officers cursed as they drove their men faster. However, the return fire had little effect, and Jonah now fully understood the commodore's concern of closing with the enemy so that the heavier firepower would be of use. At this point, the *Lawrence* was being blasted to shreds while still not in range for their big guns. Elliott's *Niagara* gave no indication of joining the battle. Jonah thought of Lieutenant Jones words, "Are we to take on the entire British squadron alone?"

For the next two hours, hell rained down on the poor *Lawrence* from the guns of the British warships, *Detroit* and *Queen Charlotte*. Jonah had never seen such destruction and yet the ship was still afloat. However, it would not remain so much longer. The Lawrence's firepower had dwindled. Most of the ship's upper works had been blasted away and still the deadly bombardment continued.

Screams, curses, and the sounds of balls plowing into the ship all seemed to mingle. The *Lawrence* was now down to seven serviceable guns, but after another devastating broadside, they were down to three.

Lieutenant J. J. Yarnell, bleeding from a bad wound to his face, ran to Perry's side. Shouting to make his voice heard, he exclaimed, "The officers in my division have all been cut down. Can I have others?"

Looking about, Perry ordered three of his own aides to assist Yarnell. Not a quarter hour later, the lieutenant was back, bleeding now from both his face and a new wound to his shoulder.

"I'm sorry, sir, but those officers have been cut down."

The sound of balls shrieking across the deck made the men duck as more cries of anguish were heard.

Perry gave a sigh then replied, "There are no more. You'll have to see the surgeon and see if any of the wounded are fit enough to fight."

"Yes sir," the lieutenant answered.

"Yarnell."

"Aye, sir."

"Have the surgeon tend to your wounds."

Men continued to fall and Jonah felt a sharp sting to his arm. Blood started to ooze. A piece of wood or metal had sliced through his shirt and caused a superficial wound. One of the riflemen quickly tied a grimy handkerchief around the wound to stop the bleeding. The men manning the last serviceable gun were now down. Perry called for help, and men crawled over the deck strewn with corpses to answer their commodore's call.

Soon, the last remaining gun was destroyed. The *Lawrence* was now so battered she was nothing more than a floating hulk. A floating hulk out of control as all the steering, sails, and rigging had been destroyed. Of one hundred thirty-six officers and men who had made up the *Lawrence's* crew, all but a dozen or so were either wounded or dead. Those left were doing all they could to care for their fallen mates. There was no one left to fight on the once beautiful ship.

Looking about, the commodore spoke grimly to the last standing lieutenant, "Find me a boat and a crew. I will transfer my flag."

"Aye, aye sir."

"Mr. Lee."

"Yes, Commodore."

"Would you care to join me?"

"My pleasure, sir."

Soon, the commodore's brother appeared with six men to row the only surviving ship's boat.

"We are ready, sir."

"Very well, haul down my banner."

As the men entered the boat, Jonah noticed two of the crew were volunteers from the Kentucky riflemen. Climbing down into the boat, Jonah winced as a pain shot through his wounded arm.

"Where to, sir?" Perry's brother asked as the commodore standing in the stern of the boat, responded using his sword as a pointer, "To the Niagara."

Rowing to the *Niagara*, Perry's boat passed close to the *Detroit*. A number of smaller weapons were fired at the boat. Canister and grape filled the air like a swarm of deadly bees. Ignoring the deadly swath, the commodore continued to stand until Jonah and a sailor persuaded him to sit. However, for all the bullets, grape, and canister fired, the commodore's luck held and the small boat passed untouched.

Breathing a sigh of relief, Jonah relaxed and silently thanked the Lord.

Chapter Thirteen

AS THE BATTLE BETWEEN the two navies ensued, Tecumseh watched from his vantage point on the shore. His leadership of the Indians was now being questioned. News of the aggressive strikes by the Southern Creeks called Red Sticks had made its way to the northern theater. The defeat of the British had many of the Indians wondering if they needed the British to fight the Americans. The Red Sticks had attacked and defeated the Americans in Alabama and massacred a settlement and Fort Mims. The American commander had been Major Daniel Beasley, who George Washington deplored and called a careless officer. Beasley had allowed the gates of Fort Mims to stay open while he played cards, ignoring the warnings he had received about the warring Red Sticks. He paid for his carelessness with his life, as he was struck down with a tomahawk as he tried in vain to close the fort's gates.

With the news of the Red Sticks victory, Tecumseh's Indians felt they no longer needed to wait on the cowardly Proctor. Tecumseh wanted to see if the British navy was braver than Proctor's army. Trying to persuade the thousands of impatient braves was proving to be difficult, and Tecumseh found he was losing control of those who desired action now. He had related that once the British had their big canoes finished and ready for battle, they would drive the Americans from the lake. Some still argued that all the British were cowards. Therefore, Tecumseh watched in anguish as the battle on the lake unfolded.

The British guns seemed to be winning, but soon after the firing started, clouds of cannon smoke as dense as fog drifted ashore destroying Tecumseh's ability to witness the battle. Soon, he could see nothing but bursts of orange flames erupting through a black haze. Tecumseh needed a British victory to maintain his position. However, as the smoke and fog of war destroyed his view, he had a sick, empty feeling in the pit of his stomach. Were his days numbered? Had he chosen to back the wrong side? Things were not as they had been when he had triumphed over the weakling William Hull.

Well, if they should be defeated, he'd not be taken alive, he decided. He would go down in battle as was fitting for a warrior. Not like the cowardly Proctor. He'd show his braves how a true warrior fought... and if need be... die.

Miraculously, Commodore Perry's boat made it to *Niagara's* side. He was met by Elliott as he climbed aboard. Expecting a blasting from the commodore, Jonah was surprised when Perry said no more than that he was taking command. Elliott congratulated the commodore on his daring in switching of ships under fire.

"He's a cool un, the sod," one of the volunteer riflemen hissed, only to receive a glare from Perry's brother.

Jonah could think of much more to say about the coward, Elliott, but held his tongue. To make matters worse, Elliott had the audacity to volunteer to bring up the other lagging boats. What surprised Jonah even more was the commodore's willingness to accept Elliott's request. *Maybe he thinks we'd be better off without him*, Jonah thought.

Elliott then climbed into the boat that had been used to carry the commodore to *Niagara* and had himself rowed over to take command of the smaller gunboats, the *Somers, Porcupine, Tigress*, and the *Trippe*. Hopefully, he'd have a better showing than was demonstrated previously. *Maybe he's embarrassed*, Jonah decided.

On board the British flagship, *Detroit*, Commander Barclay was elated to see the American commodore haul down his flag, thinking him defeated. But as bad as things had been aboard the *Lawrence*, she had gotten in her licks. Had it been balls from her carronades that found their mark or was it Perry's forward twelve-pounders? No matter, damage was done in both life and to ships. On the two largest British ships, men had paid dearly for their efforts against the *Lawrence*. The two ship's captains and lieutenants were either dead or wounded, so they were unable to fight. Barclay had been wounded in five places and was so weak he had to be taken below. The ship was then turned over to the senior surviving officer, a second lieutenant. Caring for the wounded and putting his ship back in order, the second lieutenant thought the victory had been won. He was totally unprepared for the onslaught he was about to receive from the undamaged *Niagara*.

Advancing on the British squadron Perry ordered the signals, "Make all sail and engage the enemy." Angered over the loss of life and damage to his ship, Commodore Perry sailed at the British with guns blazing. Pouring one deadly broadside after another into the *Detroit* and the *Queen Charlotte*, the *Niagara's* gunners worked as hard as they could to keep up the deadly fire. The gun captains drove the gunners without mercy in an attempt to wipe away the shame they felt from Elliott's refusal to join in the battle.

As the battle raged, the *Detroit* and *Queen Charlotte* collided. Taking advantage of the enemy blunder, Perry had a course set to bring the *Niagara* between the entangled British ships and the *Hunter*. The wind was finally in his favor and Perry meant to make the best of it. Still seething over the destruction of his *Lawrence,* the commodore showed no mercy. Perry had his guns double-shotted, with a measure of grape on top, and at point blank range raked each ship as he cut through the enemy line. Realizing he may not get such an opportunity again, Perry had the guns manned on both sides of the ship. The *Lady Prevost* felt the wrath of the port side guns while the *Detroit* and the *Queen Charlotte* received a full broadside from starboard guns.

"Fire, fire as you bear," Perry yelled after the first broadsides. Jonah was quick to understand the meaning as gun captains yelled at their crews, "Load, run out, fire. Sponge her, sponge her, blast ya lubber. Do ya want the gun to blow up in your face?"

Gun after gun leapt backward as they belched forward their fiery hell. The gunners would ram a wet swab down the barrel to extinguish any embers before another charge of powder was rammed home, followed by ball and grape. No sooner was the gun loaded than the squeal of wheels on the gun carriages would sound as men put their backs into the ropes pulling the gun back into the gun port to be fired almost instantaneously. Then the process would start all over again. Jonah noted the rags tied over the men's ears to prevent deafness. Not a single gunner seemed aware of anything or anyone else. Caked in sweat and grime, faces black from the acrid powder, the men did their job with deadly precision.

Feeling useless and in the way of the crew of the long twelve-pounder guns, Jonah made his way to a group of Kentucky volunteers. They were cutting down every available target. He watched as two men loaded while one man fired. Soon most of the men from a British gun crew were down without knowing what was happening. The long rifles didn't make as much noise as the big guns did but in the right hands they were very deadly.

Jonah had never seen such fury as the carronades belched forth utter destruction that decimated the enemy ships. The wind had also picked up, allowing the commodore's other vessels to catch up and fire into the enemy from astern. By this time, the gunboats and schooners that had entered the battle were making their mettle felt.

Jonah was both awed and frightened as the fearful battle raged with horrific fury. While the Americans were doing their utmost to defeat the British squadron, Barclay's ships were making the job most difficult. Back and forth the big guns fired. The air was rent with splinters flying; nets, riggings and yards were falling. The mast had tumbled down. Men were caught under the debris, cursing and crying out in pain. The survivors were trying to hack their way out from under the mess that fell from aloft as men died about them. Cries of pain and anger rose above the din of battle. As bad as it was on the commodore's ships, it was worse for the British. The Americans now held the upper hand. Perry seemed to be everywhere, shouting orders, directing fire and offering encouragement. Jonah had never witnessed such bravery; not only by Perry, but his entire crew. They would accept nothing less than victory...victory or death.

Unable to deal with the ferocious attack any longer, Commander Barclay surrendered in just three quarters of an hour. Several of the mildly damaged British ships tried to slip away, but the escape attempt failed as the American commanders cut them off. Once the victory was realized, the commodore stunned the surviving crewmen on board the *Lawrence* by boarding it to accept the British surrender.

Looking at Jonah, Perry said quietly, "It's only fitting after all they sacrificed."

Having his banner raised on a makeshift stanchion, the commodore looked at the masses of dead bodies and a tear fell from his eye. Jonah felt emotion swell up inside him as he looked at those who gave all to keep this country free. Well, he'd do his best to never let their deaths be in vain. That was for damn sure.

Barclay was so badly wounded he sent his senior officer to offer his apologies for his inability to move and to offer his sword. Jonah again felt himself swell with emotion as the commodore bowed and told the officer he would not accept the sword of an officer who had fought so gallantly and honorably. *Damn, I'm starting to act like an old woman,* Jonah thought.

After the ritual surrender was complete, Perry called for his chief signal officer, Lieutenant Forrest. "You are to take news to General Harrison of our victory. Mr. Lee!"

"Aye, sir," Jonah replied, proud he'd remembered the correct naval reply.

Smiling, the commodore reached into his pocket and brought out an envelope, which he tore the back off and scribbled a note. When he finished writing, he looked at Jonah and said, "Forrest here is going to deliver a message for me to General Harrison. If you wish you may accompany him ashore." The commodore then smiled after a brief pause then added, "Unless, of course, you've decided to join the Navy. If so, we'll swear you in directly."

Now it was Jonah's time to smile. "I thank you for having me, sir. I will never forget this day but I think my talents are more land based."

The two men then shook hands. After climbing down into the little boat that would take them ashore Jonah noticed Forrest staring at the note he'd been given to deliver to General Harrison.

"Interesting?" Jonah asked.

Without speaking, Forrest handed the note to Jonah. A list of ships captured was written down but what stood out was a single phrase... a phrase that said it all. As he read the phrase, the devastation of the battle between the ships at sea was at the forefront of his thoughts. The commodore had written a single, simple phrase that Jonah would never forget. ***"We have met the enemy, and they are ours."***

PART II

Chapter Fourteen

MOSES WAS WAITING WHEN Jonah made it back to Camp Seneca. Seeing how haggard Jonah looked sent a wave of concern through Moses.

"The victory did not come easy, I see," Moses stated.

Recalling the roar of cannons, the screams of pain and curses of helpless men had taken an emotional toll on Jonah. How did you explain the very hell that was all about to a person who'd never been in such a battle at sea?

"No," Jonah replied to his friend. "It did not come easy." As he recalled the number of dead men sewn into their hammocks with a cannon ball at one end and at sunset sent to the bottom of Lake Erie. No grave, no marker. Nothing but a letter to some family member informing them their loved one was gone, having made the ultimate sacrifice for his country. Fine words did little to provide for a man's family. How would they survive? That was the question on Jonah's mind.

Perry had done his part. Now it was the Army who had to press the battle. He'd not let those brave sailors and Kentucky volunteers who died such a brave death do so in vain. He would prod Harrison all the way to Canada if he had to; even it meant shoving the tip of his sword up the general's arse. Harrison would not take it kindly to being prodded but that was what the President had sent him to do. To push.

Reporting to General Harrison, Jonah found their leader to be in rare good humor. *He should be*, Jonah thought. When greetings were completed, Jonah gave his report, leaving nothing out. When he finished his narrative, he took a deep breath and spoke again.

"General, we now have the British on the run. We must push forward while they are reeling from the loss of their Navy."

"You think, if given time, they will regroup, do you?"

"Yes sir, I do. We have them on their heels, sir. It's time to put them on their backs."

"I agree with you, Jonah. I will send a rider to recall Colonel Johnson and his mounted rifles. That will add another twelve hundred men to our numbers."

"But sir," Jonah objected. "We have over four thousand men in camp now. We can mobilize them while the rider seeks out Colonel Johnson. Being mounted, they will catch up. General, I watched good men die trying to drive the British from the lakes and cut their supply line to the army. I don't think the president would be happy if we didn't take full advantage of the victory the navy paid so dearly for. The time to move, General, is now. It's time to attack the British with every man, every gun, and every blade that's at hand. They are now on the run. Let's not give them time to regroup. We must attack now."

Harrison turned red and showed his displeasure by the tone of his voice. "Well, you don't mind if I have my supper first do you, Mr. Lee? I'm sure the president would approve of a man eating before he begins a force march."

Now it was Jonah who was fuming. "I doubt he'd have the stomach for it at a time like this, General. If you don't mind, I will accompany your rider to recall Colonel Johnson." Without waiting for a reply, he wheeled around and left thinking, *I don't really give a damn whether you like it or not, I'm going.*

As he left, Jonah heard Harrison slamming down his eating utensils and barking out orders. He couldn't catch the exact words. But he didn't care; if he could push Harrison into action, damn his displeasure. He owed it to those brave sailors. Nay, he owed it to his country. Moses was drinking a cup of cider when Jonah entered the tent. Taking another cup, he filled it half full with cider then filled it the rest of the way with liquid from a stone jug, thinking it was water. Downing the fiery liquid caused Jonah to cough and his eyes to water.

"Damn, Moses! You trying to kill me?"

"No, more like putting out a fire."

"By starting a back fire," Jonah wheezed.

"If that's what it takes."

"Damn," Jonah cursed again.

"Keep that up and you're going to upset some of them Kentucky boys. They set a heap of store in what they call sipping whiskey."

"You have to sip it," Jonah said, getting his voice back. "Otherwise, it burns your throat clean through. A full cup of that downed at one time could cause a man to lose his voice forever."

Hearing this, Moses smiled and said, "There's a woman or two I might like to try that on."

"Well, I don't want to know who they are," Jonah replied. Reaching down for his bedroll, saddle, and bridle, he continued, "I'm going for a ride, want to come?"

Not waiting for an answer, Jonah shouldered his load and collided with a soldier as he walked out of the tent. "My apologies," he stated as he offered a hand to help the soldier up.

Biting back a curse, the soldier took the offered hand. "Are you Mister Lee?"

"Guilty."

Smiling at the response, the soldier's anger faded. "General Harrison is sending me after Colonel Johnson, sir. He said I was to let you know as you might prefer riding to sitting."

Another dig, Jonah thought. Well, he might have pushed a little too hard. He'd let up, but if the general wasn't ready to march when they got back, he'd find out just how hard Jonah could push.

The horses seem to understand the urgency their riders felt. Jonah kept going over and over in his mind his conversation with Harrison. He was certainly a better leader than Hull. In their days when both he and Harrison were with General Wayne, he showed no reluctance to give battle. Did he fear the unknown? Once, when they paused to give the horses a blow, Jonah discussed his concerns with Moses while the soldier led the horses down to a small creek.

"Maybe he fears death," Moses said.

"Death!" Jonah exclaimed. "Every soldier lives with that possibility. He fears something worse than death, but what could it be?"

"You can't guess?" Moses asked.

Jonah gave him a quizzical look and then replied, "You tell me."

"His soul."

Jonah was awestruck and stood spellbound for a few seconds. When he made no comment, Moses added, "No man can lead an army into battle, to kill or be killed without fearing the judgment of the Almighty."

Before Jonah could reply, the soldier was back with the horses. Deep in thought, Jonah mounted and led them off down the trail. This time the pace wasn't so hurried. It was late that afternoon when the soldier called for Jonah and Moses to hold up for a minute.

"We are almost there," the soldier muttered.

"Where?" Jonah asked.

"The River Raisin, sir. I was there when it happened."

"The massacre?" Jonah asked incredulously.

"Yes sir. I was one of the lucky ones. I had felt in my bones you couldn't trust the Redcoats, and I knew we were fools to trust the red devils. We kilt too many of the savages for them not to have devilment on their minds."

Jonah and Moses sat and waited for the soldier to speak. He was having difficulty as he relived that night in his mind. The horses stamped and pawed while they stood. Moses' horse stretched his neck, loosening the reins on the bridle. Once loose, he shook his neck and whinnied; impatiently waiting to move on or get the weight of the saddle and rider off his back.

Suddenly, the man started speaking. "We fought 'em till we was out of powder and shot, and then the major told us to fix our bayonets but then somebody surrendered. They didn't have no wagons to move the wounded on, so they was left at Frenchtown until some could be rounded up. My neighbor from back home in Ohio was one of the wounded to be carried in the wagons. When they marched off the unwounded prisoners, I ducked into the bushes and hid out. When it got dark, I was going to round him up, and if he could make it with my help, we'd skedaddle out of there back to General Harrison."

"Did you find your friend?" Jonah asked.

The soldier hung his head and shook it. "No, I never did. Once it got dark, I knew our wounded was in trouble. The red devils showed up all liquored up. Some said Proctor had it waiting on them at Stoney Creek. Whether he did or didn't, don't much matter at this time, as the killen's done been done, but if I ever get that Redcoat in my sites, he's a goner."

The soldier paused again as if recalling that night. Finally, he continued, "I wasn't the only one hiding out. I run up on a couple of boys from Kaintuck, who had the same worries I did. As more and more Indians showed up, it was plain to see they was all worked up with an appetite for blood. All night long they drank, yelled, and whooped it up. Come morning when no wagons or sleds showed up, they started their hellish ways. They had painted their faces red and black so I knew it would be a massacre. One of the Kaintuck boys wanted to high tail it, but the other was too weak, so we just stayed put. We were between some rocks that weren't too comfortable, but it was flanked by a deadfall and bushes. I figured as long as we didn't move about we'd be all right. Soon the red devils started their evil doings. They began to plunder the wounded and scalped 'em while they were at it. Some were scalped even before they were killed. Two houses full of wounded men were set afire. I don't guess I'll ever forget the smell and the screams as men were burned alive. The wounded that could took off running toward Fort Malden, but most of them were caught. They had their heads cut off and stuck on poles to put fear into the Americans. To this day, the road to Fort Malden and Frenchtown is full of bodies left to rot where they fell."

Without giving any indication he'd finished his story, the soldier clucked to his horse and rode off. Jonah felt moisture at his eyes and was surprised how emotional he'd gotten.

"Brave man," Moses volunteered.

Jonah nodded but didn't speak. The two turned their horses and rode after the lone soldier.

Chapter Fifteen

CAPTAIN CLAY GESSLIN HAD a party of skirmishers spread out when Jonah's group rode up. Stepping from behind a tree, Gesslin flagged down the riders. As they pulled up, Gesslin asked, "You pleasure riding or you got a purpose?"

Smiling, Jonah replied, "It was such a pretty day I couldn't see wasting it sitting around camp."

The soldier then saluted Gesslin. "Private Lewis, sir. I'm looking for Colonel Johnson."

"He's back at the battlefield," Gesslin said, a somber tone to his voice. "Most of those killed were Kentuckians, so the colonel felt it was time they were given a decent burial." Gesslin then called to one of his men to take charge until he returned and escorted the group to Colonel Johnson's location.

Arriving at the site where the massacre had taken place, Jonah and Moses watched from their horses as Colonel Johnson's men reverently dug graves for those bodies still intact. Johnson could be seen speaking with General Harrison's dispatch rider. The colonel then rode over to a sergeant and instructed him to finish with the graves already dug then prepare to ride out. Jonah, Moses, and Gesslin rode up to the colonel once he had given his orders.

"I hear Perry has had a great victory," Colonel Johnson volunteered.

"Yes sir," Jonah replied.

When he didn't add anything else, Johnson prompted him. "They tell me you were with Perry during the battle."

Shaking his head, Jonah gave a quick narrative of Perry's battle. When he finished, Johnson said, "A remarkable man, our commander."

"He is that," Jonah agreed. "Tried to get me to volunteer for the Navy. I respectfully declined, of course." This brought a chuckle from Johnson and Gesslin.

Colonel Johnson then asked a very direct question. "So, you think it's time to press the enemy, Mr. Lee?"

Without hesitating, Jonah replied, "I do, sir. I see no need in allowing the British to regroup. If we wait, winter will be here and that will mean we will be forced to wait until spring to engage the enemy. Who knows what they will have waiting for us by then. I feel the time is right, Colonel. We have to push now. The destiny of our nation may well depend on how fast we act."

Colonel Johnson sat staring at Jonah for a minute or so. "You and I are of one mind, sir. Let's hope we can persuade our leaders to forego too much caution and move."

"Maybe a little nudge," Gesslin spoke for the first time.

Without thinking, Jonah volunteered, "More like a kick in the arse."

Colonel Johnson bellowed out in laughter upon hearing this. "Tell me, Captain Gesslin, is Mr. Lee from Kentucky?"

"I don't think so, sir," Gesslin replied, grinning from ear to ear.

"Well, he ought to be. He speaks like a Kaintuck."

The trip back to Camp Seneca was a miserable ride. The sky grew gray as angry clouds gathered, and the wind started blowing. Then the rain started falling in sheets. Soaked clear through, the men could feel the wet cold all the way through to their bones. A couple of riders would have been able to find enough shelter to protect them from most of the weather, but with twelve hundred men, they pushed on. The horses slogged through the mud until those bringing up the rear had to struggle to get through the quagmire caused by those in the front.

Once on a stretch of high ground, the order was given to dismount. Walking, the mounted rifles gave their tired mounts a breather. After thirty minutes of walking the order was given to mount. As they rode on, Jonah heard some of the men talking. They had friends, neighbors, and relatives among the dead at the River Raisin. The grisly sight of mutilated bodies still not buried from the previous winter angered Jonah. He could only imagine the rage these men felt as they buried their friends and comrades. There would be no quarter given from this group.

General Harrison was once again in good humor when Jonah returned to camp in company with Colonel Johnson's men. An officer's call was held, and Harrison explained that he had called on Governor Shelby of Kentucky for another fifteen hundred men to help in pursuit of General Proctor.

Governor Shelby would be given the honor of leading his Kentuckians. Governor Shelby was called 'Old King Mountain' by his men. This was a tribute to the governor for his victory at King's Mountain during the first war against the British in 1780, the same year General Harrison was born. The news was music to Jonah's ears. The music was made even sweeter when he discovered a meeting was to be held the following day with Commodore Perry. He had transferred his flag to the *Ariel* and they would go aboard to map out the strategy that the combined forces would use in their attempt to defeat Proctor and the British army. After the officer's call, Jonah headed back to his tent to have a nightcap and rest his weary, achy body. Moses would be awake and hopefully he'd have something for them to eat. However, on arrival, he found Captain James Hampton and Clay Gesslin sipping bourbon from the stone jug.

Gesslin introduced Hampton to Lee and stated they'd been enjoying Moses' good cooking while they waited. *I hope there's some left,* Jonah thought.

Taking a sip of the bourbon, Gesslin looked at Jonah and asked, "Know what James does?" Not giving Jonah time to speak, he answered the question, "He handles the Canadian and Indian spies. He's got a bit of information that will plumb perk up your ears. I told him you was from Washington and would be interested in what he's found out."

"Has General Harrison been informed?" Jonah asked, wondering if the general had kept something from him.

"Oh, he'll tell the general after he's talked with Colonel Johnson."

"Colonel Johnson," Jonah repeated, not sure he was hearing right.

"Captain Hampton is from Kentucky," Gesslin said, as if that explained it all.

In fact, it did explain a lot. Jonah had already decided that most of the damn army was made up of Kaintucks. So there was little doubt where Hampton's first loyalty lay.

"How did you come to be involved with the Canadians?" Jonah asked.

"My mother, sir, is from York."

"I see. And what seems to be the attitude of the Canadians?"

Turning up his cup, Hampton drained the last of the bourbon and then stared into the empty bottom as in disbelief that it was all gone. Moses passed the jug, and Hampton poured half a cup.

"I'd say the general feeling varies considerably. Some support the Redcoats fully, others half-heartedly, but there's a bunch who want nothing to do with them and would like to see York become a part of the United States. All but the staunchest loyalist have had their fill of the Redcoats high-handed ways and taking what they want without so much as a thank you."

"I see," Jonah replied. This was much as he'd been told. "Well, Captain, what have you heard that you think will be of interest to me?"

Taking another swallow of Jonah's bourbon, Hampton replied, "It's the Indians. They are fed up with the British and are deserting in droves. Tecumseh is finding his power is weakening and has confronted Proctor openly. He's said to have compared Proctor's conduct to that of a fat animal that carries its tail on its back until trouble comes along. Then, when frightened, it tucks its tail between its legs and runs off."

"That's calling the kettle black," Gesslin volunteered. His words were a little slurred after helping himself to Jonah and Moses' jug.

"There's more," Hampton went on. "We are told Fort Malden and Amherstburg cannot be defended. Not only is there no food, but Barclay had the guns removed from the fort to be mounted on his ships so he could do battle with Commodore Perry. We're told Proctor has left his army under his second in command, Colonel Augustus Warburton, while he's packed up his wife, his personal belongings and skedaddled."

Hampton started to continue but paused as he let go a long and loud belch. "Pardon me!" he exclaimed, reaching for the jug once more only to find Gesslin had already drained the last of its contents. "Had to happen sooner or later," he mused.

"What?" Jonah asked

"The well has gone dry," Hampton answered, as he belched again. When he took a deep sigh but didn't continue, Jonah prompted him.

"You were saying?"

"Saying," Hampton repeated, his eyes now looking heavy and glassy. "Oh, yes. We were told Proctor has promised Tecumseh he'll make a stand. However, our sources don't know when or where the stand will be."

Chapter Sixteen

A FEW DAYS LATER, THE decision was made to go after the British from two fronts. Colonel Johnson would go over land with his mounted rifles, while the infantry would be transported on Commodore Perry's ships. For two days, beginning on September 25th, Perry transported the army to a forward position. Seeing the American warships caused a panic among those loyal to the British, as their army had fled, leaving no one to protect them.

Harrison's troops were put ashore in small boats at a landing some three miles below Fort Malden called Hartley Point. Expecting the worst, Perry had loaded and run out his cannons should a covering fire be needed. There was little need, however, as the army landed without being fired upon by cannon or musket. Sending out an advance party, they came upon a farmer's wife. She attempted to run but was quickly cut off. Once she realized her captors were not looking to harm her but only wanted information, she quickly told them how just the day before, Proctor's army had retreated.

She went on to say they had burned most of the public buildings and destroyed everything they thought the Americans might use, including all the food they couldn't carry with them. The lieutenant sent a dispatch back to General Harrison. When he came ashore, he had his drums and fifes playing "Yankee Doodle." The British army had retreated until they were now back on Canadian soil.

Expecting Harrison to immediately set out in pursuit of the British, his officers were astonished when the general made no attempt to hurry after the enemy. Entering Amherstburg at the head of his army,

Harrison seemed content and relieved he'd been spared a battle. The charred remains of Fort Malden stood silent and eerie. Would it have been different if Barclay hadn't stripped the fort of its guns? More than one soldier glared upon the ruins as they passed it.

"Sir... General Harrison, sir."

Turning to see who was addressing him, Harrison found Captain Hampton with one of the city's residents. *One of Hampton's spies most likely*, Harrison thought. "What is it, Captain?"

"I have word, sir that Tecumseh has just left. If you take my glass, you can see him sitting astride his horse on yonder hill."

Taking the offered glass, the general fiddled with the focus then replied, "Yes, I see him. He's just sitting there... watching."

"Shall we send a squad after him, sir?"

"No, Captain. He would be gone before you could get out of town."

"We could try, sir."

"No, Captain. Return this man to his home and then go back to your unit."

"Yes sir," Hampton replied dejectedly.

When Harrison finally gave the word to move out, he decided it would not be good to leave the city without a force to keep control should the British or Indians return.

Departing on September 28th, it took two days to reach Sandwich, just eighteen miles away. Sandwich was located just across the strait from Detroit. Once there, Harrison lay over three days waiting on Colonel Johnson's mounted rifles to join up. While waiting, Harrison ignored his seething officers and took over the home of Colonel James Baby, which had also been the headquarters of William Hull, the disgraced American commander.

Letting his horse crop at a small patch of grass, Jonah watched as Harrison's infantry climbed into the boats to be rowed back out to Commodore Perry's ships. His reverie was broken as Captain Clay Gesslin rode up.

Nodding to Moses, Gesslin spoke to Jonah. "The colonel is ready to pull out."

"Looks like they might have a wet ride," Jonah said, referring to the soldiers in the boats.

"Better them than us," Gesslin replied, using his head to indicate the loading of the infantry.

"I won't argue," Jonah said. "How about you, Moses, land or sea?"

"I'll stick to this hoss. If he goes down, I can still walk. One of them ships go down, I'd be in a heap of trouble. Only one man I ever heard of who could walk on water, and I never been much at swimming." As an afterthought, Moses added, "And I certainly can't drink that much water." This brought a chuckle from Jonah and Gesslin.

"I like his thinking," Gesslin said, as the three of them swung their horses around to catch up to the colonel.

"Glad to see you, Mr. Lee," Colonel Johnson greeted Jonah as they rode up. "I don't believe you've had the pleasure of meeting my brother, have you?"

"No sir."

"James, this is Mr. Jonah Lee. He has the confidence of the president. Mr. Lee, my brother, Lieutenant Colonel James Johnson. He is my second in command."

As the two shook hands, Jonah felt firmness in the man's grip and decided he, like his brother, would be a formidable opponent.

"It's good to meet you," James said. "I've seen you in camp and Clay speaks highly of you."

By the use of Gesslin's first name, Jonah decided James was a little more relaxed than his brother.

Captain Gesslin was assigned the forward detail. Thinking it would be a cooler ride, Jonah and Moses decided to accompany the group. As much as Gesslin's Kentucky volunteers liked to whoop it up in camp, they were all business on the trail.

About noon, a heavy mist began to fall; not a heavy rain, not even a sprinkle, just a mist. As the group rode toward Detroit, Jonah realized a man would have his hands full trying to make a go of it in this area. The country seemed low and soggy. They passed a few frame houses and a couple of larger houses with barns in the back. However, they were all deserted. Not a single soul was sighted, not even an Indian.

"You ever been to Detroit?" Gesslin asked as he sidled his horse next to Jonah's.

"No, I've not had that pleasure," Jonah responded.

"It's a sight different than this area," Gesslin explained. "Not barren like you see here. The town is laid out regular- like into streets and even alleys. I expect they have one hundred and fifty homes. The land is more level and the farms produce good crops. Mostly orchards and wheat; it's too cold for corn. Most folks in the town are American, but a few Canadians are about. The Detroit River has a lot of traffic. At one place, it's a mile wide." Gesslin seemed to ignore the mist as he talked and rode. He did have a small hide draped over his long rifle to keep the firing pan dry.

As the group rounded a bend, Gesslin's point rider had pulled up. "Small Indian village up ahead," he volunteered as Gesslin, Jonah, and Moses rode up. "Smoke coming from some of the huts, so I guess somebody is minding the fire."

"Huh," Gesslin snorted. "They have better sense than we do, at least they're inside."

Ignoring his captain's comments, Coot, the scout, dug into his leather pouch and came out with a plug of tobacco. Unwrapping the brown paper from around the plug, Coot then brushed and blew away any dirt or lint. Being polite, he held out the plug for anyone to take a chew. When nobody reached for the plug, he stuck it in his mouth and tore off a chew.

"Don't blame you," he volunteered when everyone passed. "It's been known to turn a man's innards."

Gesslin seemed as patient as Job as he waited for the man to work his cud then spit.

That done, Coot wiped his chin on his sleeve and said, "They's a marsh to one side of the huts. No way to go around, as I can see. Have to pass the huts."

This was what Gesslin had been waiting for. He knew his man and gave him time to make his report. Signaling to one of the other riders, Gesslin wrote a quick note to be carried to Colonel Johnson.

As the messenger galloped off, Gesslin spoke. "Let's get a better view of this village."

The group followed the trail a ways, but when the smell of smoke was distinct, they eased into the woods. After a hundred yards or so, the village was in plain sight. The huts were made out of tree branches and mud. Smoke rose from a few crude chimneys but not a soul was in sight. There was no sound, not a child crying, or a dog barking, not even a horse was seen.

"I don't like it," Jonah whispered.

"Me neither," Gesslin responded. "Let's get out of here."

Chapter Seventeen

A BLOODCURDLING YELL FILLED THE stillness, followed by bodies painted in war paint dropping onto the riders from the trees.

As Captain Gesslin was hurled to the ground by his assailant, he shouted, "Ride for help."

One of the riders at the rear of the detail caught a glancing blow on the shoulder from a tomahawk. He blasted his foe at point blank range with his rifle, then dug his heels into his mount and bounded away.

Meanwhile, Jonah was trying to rise from the ground where he was pinned by one Indian while another was tugging at the rifle held firmly in his hand. Seeing his friend, Clay, about to be stabbed with a wicked-looking knife, Jonah pulled the trigger of his rifle causing the one Indian to fall backwards from the impact of the ball. Rolling, he pulled his own knife and quickly dispatched his other foe. Reaching out, he grasped the Indian who was trying to kill his friend. Twisting the Indian's arm, Jonah struck with all of his might plunging his blade deep into the kidney of the brave. The Indian fell forward dead. Another Indian had snatched up Gesslin's gun and pointed the recovered rifle at Jonah. Kicking out, Jonah caught the Indian just below the knee, dislocating it. The rifle went off as the Indian fell. Hearing a thud and feeling a jerk, it took a moment to realize the ball had struck a dead branch causing it to fall into Jonah. Standing, Jonah could see Moses was backed against a tree with two of the red devils closing in.

Picking up a tomahawk Jonah charged forward and buried it in the skull of one of the attackers. Seeing his friend fall, the second Indian turned to face this new challenge. Too late, he realized his mistake as Moses grabbed a handful of hair and deftly pulled his sharp blade across the exposed throat. A gurgling noise was heard as the Indian dropped.

Turning to see how his comrades were making out, a sick feeling came over Jonah as one of the Indians scalped Coot, who let out a scream. Picking up his rifle, Jonah clubbed the Indian from behind and hit him a couple more times with the metal butt plate, turning the Indian's skull into a bloody pulp.

A shot rang out. Whirling around, Jonah saw an Indian go down kicking while Gesslin held a smoking pistol in his hand. Blood oozed from a cut to his scalp and to his shoulder. But he was alive and fighting. Jonah gave a sigh of relief. He'd come to really like Gesslin and would take it hard if he fell. As quick as the attack had begun, it was over.

"Damn," Gesslin swore, as he looked about. One man dead with a tomahawk still buried in his back. Coots, wounded and scalped, and still another; the one who rode away for help was wounded, but how bad was still to be seen.

Moses had a huge goose egg knot over his temporal area and a busted lip. Jonah's ribs hurt so bad, it was hard to take a breath.

"Damn," Gesslin cursed again. "I let my men get ambushed like some bunch of city folks."

"You're not the only one," Jonah said, trying to salve his friend's hurt.

"But I was in charge."

"Makes no never mind, Clay. You did everything right. You took every precaution. This is war and men die." Placing his hand on his friend's shoulder, he continued, "It could have been worse."

"Tell him that," Gesslin replied, pointing to the scalped Coot.

"He's alive," Jonah started to say but remained silent.

Moses walked over and took the scalp from the dead Indian's hand. He then rinsed it off with water from his canteen. With Jonah and Gesslin watching, he poured water over the wounded man's head, and then placed the scalp back over the wound. He adjusted it slightly, then tore a strip from a blanket and bound it over the scalp and under the jaw

"Don't try to talk," he cautioned Coot. Then as an afterthought, he added, "Leave your chew in the pouch."

Once clear of the wounded man, Jonah asked, "Will that grow back?"

Nodding, Jonah went to look for a small flask he carried in his saddlebag. He could use a drink, and Coot could probably use the whole bottle. Taking a swallow, the sound of Colonel Johnson's men could be heard. Maybe they'd have a jug somewhere.

Skirmishers were sent out and the small village was quickly searched. A British officer's coat was found but little more. The huts were destroyed and the group pulled out. Later that night, Gesslin stopped by Jonah and Moses' camp. Moses had managed to get a fire going in spite of the dampness.

"Pine knot, what some call lighter, will burn every time," Moses was telling one of the men. "I always keep a few sticks in my possible bag for days like this."

Soon, the aroma of hot coffee could be smelled all over the camp. After taking the cup of offered coffee, Gesslin squatted next to the fire.

"Thanks for being supportive this afternoon," he half-whispered. "The colonel said as much." Pausing to blow on the strong black liquid, Gesslin took a timid sip then added, "The sawbones said Moses may have prevented ill vapors and purification by fixing Coot up like he did. Says he'll probably still be bald on top."

"Did he take the ah... scalp off?" Moses asked.

"No, said to leave it there where it belongs."

"Is the same bandage still on?"

"No," Gesslin chuckled. "They handed a bottle of brandy to Coot, who drank it down. He'd already had a nip from somebody's jug. Soon he was snoring away. The sawbones took the opportunity to put on a clean bandage while he slept. Now he looks like he's got a toothache or something. He'll have a headache come tomorrow, I'm betting."

"Of that I'm certain," Jonah said, causing those around him to chuckle.

The rest of the trip was uneventful. They passed more deserted homes and one more deserted Indian village.

"Once the British pulled out, the red devils didn't have anyone to protect them so they lit out as well," Lieutenant Colonel James Johnson theorized. "They'll pay for their hellish ways, though, of that I'm certain."

The weather was clear for the rest of the journey, but now that it was early October, the mornings and evenings had a definite chill that seemed to last longer each day. Jonah despaired more and more over bringing the British to battle before the winter came. As the cold set in, the mood of the men changed. What once made them laugh now made them snarl and curse. They were all bone tired and saddle sore when they came to the River Rouge. Here, Johnson's men made camp and waited for Harrison's messenger. A full day's rest was a balm for the men.

The next morning, a Captain Sympson arrived with the news that General Harrison's forces were about five miles up the Detroit River at Sandwich. After a hearty breakfast the regiment saddled up and moved out to rendezvous with the general.

Riding into General Harrison's camp was much different than on previous occasions. The mood in the camp was very somber. There was none of the good-natured jabs thrown at the mounted rifles by the infantry. There was also no hooting and hollering that usually existed at this time of day when the army was in camp.

Moses edged his horse up next to Jonah and half-whispered, "Something is going on... something serious."

"Do you think it's the knowledge we'll soon come to battle with the British?" Jonah asked, knowing Moses had a feeling for such matters.

"No... I don't think that's it. Most of these boys would be hunting liquid courage and bragging about how many Redcoats and red devils they planned to plant."

Recognizing a recent acquaintance, Jonah and Moses rode over to where Captain James Hampton stood under a huge old walnut tree.

"Jonah," the captain spoke, touching his hat in greeting. "You and Moses made it through with your scalps, I see. I did hear you had a mite of trouble."

Now, how in the hell did he know that, Jonah wondered.

"Wasn't much trouble," Moses commented. "Not so much as to create notice."

Hearing this, Captain Hampton raised his eyebrow as if to say, that's not what I heard.

Jonah, then using Hampton's first name, asked, "What is going on, James? It seems we've ridden into a sullen camp."

"Firing squad will make things that way."

"Was somebody shot?" Jonah inquired, not sure he'd heard Hampton correctly.

"Not yet," the captain replied. "But will be in the morning at first light."

"What for? What was his offense?" Jonah muttered.

"Desertion, third time in fact."

"Damn," Jonah swore. "That's not good with a battle looming in the near future."

"Well, it sends a message," Hampton countered. "Ain't nobody in this army that didn't sign up on his own free will. But once you sign, you're bound by the regulations. Sides, he was told after his second time what would happen if he ran again. Brought it on himself, I reckon."

Jonah looked at Moses, who just shook his head and whispered, "May the Lord be with him."

As the two started off, Hampton called after them. "Rider came in today. There's mail and dispatches at the general's headquarters." He then gave directions to where the headquarters had been set up. Thanking Hampton again, Jonah and Moses rode away.

"Hopefully, we will find that headquarters has a place assigned for us," Jonah said, still feeling low over the news from Hampton.

Thunder rolled in the east and gray clouds were building. A corporal was in front of the general's headquarters when Jonah and Moses rode up.

"There's a small barn out back where your horses will be safe," the corporal volunteered. He'd been around the general's staff enough to know Jonah was the president's man and was to be offered every courtesy.

Thanking the corporal, the men kicked the mud and dirt off their boots and made their way to the front door of a large comfortable-looking house. A bright crack of lightning followed by a loud boom made Moses jump.

"That was close," he swore. "Made my hair stand up."

Jonah couldn't help but smile at Moses' discomfort. Then the rain began to pour... a heavy downpour.

"Might rain out the firing squad," Jonah commented.

Shaking his head, Moses replied, "No. We'll have a let-up tomorrow morning for a while, and then I expect it'll be with us a few days."

"I hope not," Jonah replied.

"Wanna bet on it?" Moses smirked.

Jonah's reply was just a stare.

Chapter Eighteen

CAPTAIN CHARLES TODD, GENERAL Harrison's aide, met Jonah and Moses as they entered the headquarters. "Mr. Lee, Moses. It is good to see you."

"Captain," Jonah and Moses replied in greeting.

"The general is talking with Governor Shelby, Commodore Perry, General Cass, and General Clay. They are expecting Colonel Johnson at any time. Mr. Lee, General Harrison has left word that you are welcome to join them, sir."

Humm! Jonah thought for a second, and then asked, "Is this a social gathering, Captain, or are they meeting to discuss battle plans to engage the British?"

"I wouldn't know for certain, sir," Todd replied, then looked about to see if anyone was watching or within hearing distance. Seeing no one, Todd leaned forward and spoke; his voice barely above a whisper. "With the amount of food and strong spirits that has been ordered, sir, I can hardly see any battle plans being set in place. Might be hard enough to reset a cork."

This brought a smile from both Jonah and Moses. "I'll think on it, Captain. Moses and I need to find quarters first and Captain Hampton informed me there was mail and dispatches waiting."

"Yes sir, they are." Then, leaning toward Jonah, Todd lowered his voice again, "It appears there are letters from Washington, sir. From both the secretary of war and the president." A smile crept across Todd's face as he continued, "The general was about to bust a gut with curiosity when he learned about the letters."

"Learned from whom, Captain?" Jonah asked, with firmness in his voice.

"I dunno, Mr. Lee. That's the God's honest truth. Whoever told him had left when I came in."

Jonah softened a bit, seeing how nervous his question had made Todd. "Well, Captain, if you will be so kind, would you go fetch my mail? Moses and I still have to find quarters and this rain doesn't appear to be letting up."

"Yes sir. Oh, Mr. Lee, behind the main house is a small building that was used by the servants when Colonel Baby occupied this... ah, dwelling."

"I see. We'll look at it. Now for my mail."

"Yes sir."

When Todd returned with a courier pouch with the Presidential Seal emblazoned on it, Jonah couldn't help but muse. *No wonder Harrison was about to bust a gut.* Todd handed him several other letters as well. One of which he recognized right off as being from his mother.

Handing the mail to Jonah, Todd led him and Moses down a hall and out a rear door onto a covered back porch. The rain was still pouring down; the water gushing off the roof like Niagara Falls. The backyard was already like a lake.

"Wet shoes for sure," Moses muttered. "Not that it'll matter, as we'll likely drown getting to the little cottage."

Todd bid the two a good afternoon but stopped when Jonah laid his hand on his shoulder.

"Am I to understand, Captain, the place is ready to be used? Beds, blankets, candles, a stove or fireplace, and wood?"

"Well, sir, I was told it was."

Gazing at the sky and pouring rain, Jonah said, "I'll not be happy if I get soaked running to yonder quarters and find it to be in need."

Swallowing hard, the captain said, "I'll be right back, sir."

When he returned, he had his slicker on, and a rolled up blanket. A candle could be seen protruding from one end of the blanket. As Todd dashed off the porch, Moses turned to go back inside.

"Where are you going?" Jonah inquired.

"We passed a kitchen. I'm going to see what is to be had. No use going out again in this, unless we have to." Moses returned with a heavy sack that clinked.

"I see you've found beverage as well."

"Man should not eat bread alone," Moses replied.

Out in the cabin, a dim light was visible through one of the windows. The door opened spilling more light into the yard. Todd, with his cloak up over his head, paused in the doorway momentarily. Seeing no let up in the downpour, he gathered up his nerve and made a dash for the back porch where Jonah and Moses stood. As Todd neared the porch, a cat that had been under the porch floor must have smelled the food in Moses' sack. The cat meowed and jumped to the steps just as Todd's boot hit the bottom plank. Frightened, the cat let out a startled screech. The screech caused Todd to try to stop but his boot slid on the wet step causing him to fall backwards. With nothing to grab on to he landed with a splat. The deluge off the roof poured on to the prostrate man's midsection.

"Damn that cat," he sputtered as Jonah rushed to his aid.

"Are you all right, Captain?"

Slowly, Todd rose up. "Right enough to kill that cat, Mr. Lee."

Looking toward the porch the cat could not be seen. "Jumped off the porch," Moses volunteered.

Helping Todd back on the porch, Jonah pulled at his soggy clothing.

"I'm sorry you got wet, sir," Todd apologized, still looking the worse from his spill. "If you have no further need of me, I will go change my uniform." Pools of water were gathering at the captain's feet from the soaked uniform.

"Were I you, Captain, I'd take off the uniform out here," Jonah advised. "Otherwise, you are sure to track up the floor."

"I'll go get a blanket," Moses volunteered, still holding the bag of food firmly.

"Thank you sir, that would be most kind," Todd responded, shivering now that the air was getting cooler.

Once the captain was taken care of, Jonah looked over to Moses. "Ready," he said.

Moses bent over and picked up the captain's forgotten cloak. As he pulled it over his shoulders and head, he said, "Ready."

Glaring at his friend, Jonah sarcastically asked, "What makes you so special that you get the cloak?"

Moses smiled and quipped, "Cause you're already wet."

Then before Jonah could speak, Moses bounded off the porch and ran to what he called the little cottage. Staring at his friend's back, Jonah sighed and took off after him.

The little cottage was snug and dry. The captain had lit a small fire to help remove the dampness. The kindling was fresh, but the firewood had been there for awhile. Dust could be seen everywhere. Over in the corner, somebody had piled their bedrolls and possible bag. Jonah stripped down to his long-handles and pulled a chair up close to the fire. His boots sat on the hearth to one side, while his sodden clothes, which were draped over a straight-back chair steamed from the fireplace heat.

"Do you reckon they will be ready to wear tomorrow?" Jonah asked.

Moses looked through the small doorway from the kitchen. Seeing the steam rising off the clothes, he chuckled and replied, "If they ain't shrunk."

Paying heed to Moses' comments, Jonah slid the chair back a foot or so. Moses had found dishes in a cupboard and piled two plates high with chicken, fresh bread, and cheese. Handing Jonah a plate, he set the other on a chair next to Jonah's and then went back into the kitchen, returning with two glasses and a bottle of wine.

Seating himself, he looked over at Jonah and said, "There is plenty if you need more, plus there's a cherry pie if you've a taste for sweets after."

A piece of chicken was halfway to his mouth when Jonah paused. "Did you leave any for the general's supper?" When he didn't hear a reply, Jonah turned to Moses with a look and said, "Well?"

Moses finished chewing, swallowed, and then took a swallow of wine to wash his food down. "I really wasn't thinking of the general but there should be enough. If not, he's got servants." Pausing, a twinkle filled Moses' eyes and he spoke again, "Course, now if you're worried, you can pack up what is left and take it back to the kitchen."

When Jonah didn't reply, Moses said, "Well?"

Jonah yawned, got up from his chair and stretched. The fire was low so he threw another insect eaten piece of firewood on the fire. He took his boots off the hearth and turned his clothes over. They were almost dry now. Hearing a familiar sound, he turned. Moses was asleep on one of the small beds. The heat, full belly, and a couple of glasses of wine had him out... snoring, but out. Jonah walked over to the door and looked out. The rain had slacked up some but had not stopped. He felt a chill as a small breeze blew the damp cold air through the open doorway. Closing the door quickly, Jonah walked back over to the fire.

The sudden chill seemed to punctuate Armstrong's letter. He didn't seem pleased that the British had not been brought to a conclusive battle. Winter was setting in, and the Americans needed the northwest retaken before winter. The president had encouraged Jonah to use his authority to gently push at every opportunity. Jonah couldn't help but wonder who else was supplying information back to Washington. *Was it Colonel Richard Mentor Johnson? He was known in Congress as a war hawk. Was Johnson sending private dispatches? Was he receiving private dispatches?* Thinking back when Clay Gesslin had introduced Jonah to James Hampton, they let it slip Hampton would speak to Johnson before reporting to General Harrison.

Feeling his eyes grow heavy, Jonah placed another small stick of firewood on the fire then crawled into bed. Sleep was elusive, however. His mind was still on his letters. The secretary of war was concerned about the British influence in the south. Armstrong had mentioned in his letter of trouble in the south... Indian trouble. Problems with the Red Sticks or the Creeks as some called them. They were playing havoc among the settlers. The folks in Alabama were in need of help but with the war ongoing in the northwest, the ability to send help was limited.

If the British could be quickly defeated in the northwest, then resources could be funneled to the south. Trying to not worry about his home, Jonah rolled over. His last thoughts were, *I wonder if John Armstrong has bitten off more than he bargained for accepting the office of Secretary of War.* Then, as an afterthought, he wondered, *what have I gotten myself into?*

Chapter Nineteen

A BREAK IN THE RAIN came at dawn the next morning. Moses was first out of bed, so he added some kindling to the few remaining coals in the fireplace. Soon a small tendril of smoke started rising, then flames. Once the kindling was going good, Moses added a few sticks of firewood. The box holding the firewood was low. If they stayed tonight it would have to be replenished. It would be a good trick to find dry firewood after the gully washer they had last evening. Maybe they had a woodshed. Putting on his boots, Moses looked to the sleeping figure still in his bed.

"Get up, lazy bones." Getting both boots on, Moses shook Jonah's bed, "Get up!"

"Why?"

"Cause I'm going to get some coffee."

"All right."

As Moses turned to go, he saw the letters on a small table. The candle was down to not much more than a nub. Jonah had been up going over the letters from home.

Turning his attention back to the bed, Moses shook it hard. Jonah quickly spoke, "I'm getting up."

Moses smiled and asked, "Everybody at home making out?"

"They've got their ailments but didn't mention anything worrisome."

Now, Moses chuckled. You didn't ask Mama Lee how she was doing unless you had a good half hour. Saying no more, Moses ducked out the door and Jonah rose. The room was cool compared to the warm bed. Standing by the fireplace, he dressed hurriedly. His boots were tight-fitting from drying out next to the fire the last evening. Hopefully, they would stretch out without having to wet them.

A bump at the door was heard. Opening it, Jonah found Moses waiting with his hands full. Helping his friend, Jonah was awed at how much Moses had carried. He had a plate with eggs and bacon, another with butter biscuits, a jar of grape preserves, and a pot of coffee. Moses had always had a knack as a forager. "It's the Indian in him," Jonah's father had once said. "Good thieves, all of them."

Smiling, as he recalled his father's words, Jonah had to think quickly when Moses asked, "What are you smiling about?"

"This breakfast," Jonah replied. "It would be hard for a wife to compete with you, Moses."

"Huh! Some thangs wouldn't be no competition. Sides, as lazy as you are, ain't likely you'd find a woman who'd have you; not for long, anyway."

Biting into a butter biscuit, Jonah asked, "You see anybody? Are they up and moving?"

"The cook said the general had just left. Say's everyone has to be on hand for the firing squad."

Neither spoke for a moment or two when Moses broke the silence. "Glad I ain't in the army on days like this."

Nodding his agreement, Jonah took a sip of coffee. So was he.

After breakfast, Jonah and Moses loaded all the dishes in the empty sack Moses had used the previous evening and carried them to the kitchen. Several cats ran across the muddy yard, so Jonah dumped the few scraps they had for them. His feet ached from his tight boots.

"I think I'll take a walk to see if I can stretch these boots," Jonah said as Moses climbed the steps to the back porch.

Nodding, Moses went into the house. He'd check for firewood after he gave the dishes to the cook.

In the distance, the unmistakable drum roll was heard. It was followed by the report of rifles fired in unison. *It's done,* Jonah thought. *What kind of letter would be written to this man's family?*

The sun was starting to peek through the clouds and rays glared off the river in spots. Having the upcoming battle with the British on his mind and thinking of the Indian troubles in Alabama, Jonah walked further than he realized. *It must be mid-morning,* he thought as he turned to make his way back toward Sandwich. He had followed the river bank as he walked but decided it would be closer to walk back through town. The houses were mostly of frame, but toward the center of town, Jonah could see a few brick dwellings. As he walked down the main street, he heard a curse, a slapping sound, and a woman scream. Jonah paused for a second and then heard another scream from inside a small house that was in front of him.

Jumping over a small fence, he entered an open door. A woman was being attacked. Her attacker had his back to Jonah. As the man raised his hand to strike the woman again, Jonah grabbed it, spinning the man around and slapping him. The force of the blow sent the man to the floor. Surprised, the man touched his stinging face and then made a motion to pull his sword. The click of the hammer being pulled back on Jonah's pistol made the man freeze.

"You have me at a disadvantage, sir," he spat but made no attempt to rise.

"As you had the lady," Jonah replied.

"She deserved what she got and more," the man hissed. "She's nothing but a British tart."

"Liar... you lying scum," the woman threw back.

"I had no choice. You... you ran and hid in the woods."

The man started to speak again, but Jonah shouted, "That's enough." Then, looking at the man, he motioned with his pistol to get up.

Still touching his stinging face, the man said, "You will pay for this."

"By whom?" Jonah exclaimed. "A man who slaps around defenseless women. I think not."

"But she is a traitorous bit…" the man's sentence was broke off as Jonah's pistol was jammed into his face.

"Don't say it," Jonah warned.

Hatred filled the man's blazing eyes, but he was not foolish enough to finish his sentence. The two glared at each other for a moment. Finally, Jonah lowered the pistol.

"You have insulted me," the man spoke calmly, the hint of a French accent in his voice.

"As you have the lady," Jonah flung back.

Whatever went through the man's mind remained unspoken until he took a deep breath and bowed. "My name is Jacques LeRoche. I demand satisfaction. If you are a gentleman, you will know what I mean."

"I know what you mean," Jonah replied, disgust in his voice. "As I see it, the lady is the one who has been insulted. Any man who would strike a lady is totally without honor and could hardly be called a gentleman."

LeRoche, hearing this, gasped with fury and once again his hand went to the hilt of his sword.

"Go ahead," Jonah snapped. "Pull that blade and I'll shoot you down like the dog you are."

Taking several deep breaths, LeRoche said, "Where will my second be able to find you?"

"Do you know of Colonel Baby's house?" Jonah asked.

"I do."

"I will be there. If you insist upon this, your man had better be there soon," Jonah said, "as I'm not sure when we will march."

"He will be there within the hour."

"I will be waiting."

Once the man left, the woman said, "I thank you, sir, but you don't know what you have done. LeRoche is a ruthless man. He has killed many men with both his pistol and his blade."

"I could not allow him to hit you," Jonah said, suddenly feeling tired, now that the anger had subsided.

"He would have beaten me... but he will kill you, sir."

"I think not," Jonah replied, wishing he felt as sure as he spoke. "Now, gather a few of your things. I'm not going to leave you here for him to harm you."

The woman quickly gathered a few belongings and the two of them made their way back to the headquarters. The first person Jonah saw was Captain Todd.

"Good morning, Captain."

"And to you, sir," the young man replied, his eyes taking in the beautiful woman next to Jonah.

Seeing the obvious look of desire fill the young officer's face, Jonah realized he'd been so preoccupied, he'd not really looked at the woman.

"Is Moses about, Captain?"

"I've not seen him, sir."

"I see...Well, Captain, would you loan me your sergeant for a quick errand?"

"Yes sir, I will see if he's about. If not, will the corporal do?"

"Either will do, Captain. Just send one of the two to my quarters."

A smile was now on the captain's face. Jonah had started down the hall toward the back. Seeing the smile, he stopped.

"Wait here," he said to the woman, and then he retraced his steps to where the captain still stood. Leaning forward, he whispered, "Close your mouth, Captain, you are drooling."

Turning red, Todd closed his mouth.

"I was only joking," Jonah said.

"Ah..." Todd started but didn't finish. He did relax though.

"Any word on marching orders?" Jonah asked.

"Yes sir, in the morning, first light."

"Thank you, Captain," Jonah said, as he turned and walked away.

Chapter Twenty

AS THE TWO WALKED off the back porch toward the little cabin, Jonah caught a whiff of the woman's hair. It had been freshly washed, probably earlier that morning, as the scent of soap was still present. As he walked across the yard, Jonah found himself hoping Moses was out. He would like to spend some time alone with this rare beauty of a woman. Never had a pair of eyes moved him so much. They were a deep blue with thick lashes. The woman's skin was tanned from being outside so much. She had full lips and her hair was almost a blue-black color and hung heavy and thick about her shoulders. Her dress was a simple off-white cotton dress. The neckline was open, revealing a graceful slim throat beneath which ample breasts stretched the material. She had a simple sash tied about her middle that accented her small waist. When she stepped to one side to allow Jonah to open the cabin door, her hair moved just enough to show a turquoise earring.

Opening the door, Jonah stood in silence and stared as she gracefully eased by him and entered the cabin. The flames of desire were so strong, he felt his heart racing and blood pounding in his temples.

Light from the windows did little for the dark interior so Jonah lit a candle and muttered, "Would you like to be seated?"

As the woman sat in one of the two chairs, Jonah said, "My apologies, madam. I have failed to properly introduce myself. I'm Jonah Lee."

Smiling, she replied, "I'm Anastasia Greenville."

"At your service," Jonah replied and gave a bow. Seeing Anastasia smile, he realized how ridiculous he must look and suddenly they were both laughing.

"Do you often go looking for damsels in distress so that you may come to their rescue?"

Seeing the twinkle in Anastasia's eyes, Jonah replied, "Only when they are as beautiful as you."

"A gallant man who also knows how to flatter a woman." There was a hint of French in her accent which made Jonah wonder if she was French Canadian.

"You're French?" he asked.

"My mother," she replied. "Her family were Huguenots, who preferred to leave France rather than change religious beliefs."

Jonah knew very little about Huguenots, but decided he'd find out more about them.

"My mother married an American from Detroit, so I guess I'm an American now," she continued.

"Anastasia...is that French?" Jonah asked.

Nodding, she replied, "Yes, it was my grandmother's name." A knock at the door interrupted the conversation.

"Enter," Jonah sang out, embarrassing himself. The gentlemanly thing to do would have been to get up and answer the door. It was the sergeant.

"Captain said you wanted to see me, sir."

"Yes, Sergeant. Do you know Captain Clay Gesslin?"

"Yes sir, he's one of Colonel Johnson's officers."

"Yes, that's him," Jonah said. "Would you be so kind as to find him quickly and let him know if it's convenient that he should call on me? It's an urgent matter, Sergeant."

Looking from Jonah to Anastasia and back to Jonah, the sergeant replied, "Sir, he's with that spy in the general's headquarters right now."

By using the term 'spy,' Jonah guessed the sergeant meant James Hampton. However, he wished he'd not called the man such in front of Anastasia. Everything seemed to be on the up and up, but who knew? *Up and up*, Jonah thought. *How the devil do I know? She may well be a British spy herself. A damn pretty one if she is.*

"You did what?"

"Shhh..."

Clay Gesslin stared at his friend in disbelief. He then looked at the grandfather clock ticking in the corner. "You know the general has forbidden dueling among his officers."

"I'm not worried," Jonah answered his friend, seeing the alarm his news had caused him.

"Well, I am," Gesslin offered and then gave a sigh.

"Technically, I'm not one of his officers, therefore the general's rule of dueling does not apply to me," Jonah mumbled, not wanting to cause trouble for his friend.

"Humph," Gesslin snorted. "But it does apply to me."

"Ah...I've not been asked," Hampton interrupted the two, "but I would probably be a better choice as a second." He had overheard the entire conversation and decided to rescue Gesslin, who was obviously out of his element.

"How so?" Gesslin asked before Jonah could open his mouth.

"While I do hold a commission, it's more for convenience. I'm not really a serving officer but more an agent for the war department," Hampton replied. "Also, not only did I take fencing in school, but I have been involved in a duel or two previously."

As Jonah and Gesslin look at Hampton in disbelief, he quickly added, "Nothing more than trifling matters really. More to the point, if I was asked, I would be pleased to act as your second, Mr. Lee."

"Oh yes, by all means... that is, if you don't mind, Clay?"

"Oh no, I'll bow to experience." While his words sounded disappointed, the look of relief was also obvious.

"Good, it's settled then. Now, Mr. Lee, if you don't mind, I shall instruct certain friends of mine to make inquiries into Mr. LeRoche's background. We will also see if there is any basis for his remarks and behavior toward the lady, Anastasia."

It's amazing, Jonah thought. How the other night Hampton was just one of the boys from Kentucky. And here in the last few minutes, he had shown a completely different side of himself. This led Jonah to think his earlier thoughts were correct. There probably was a connection between Colonel Mentor Johnson, the war hawk congressman, and Hampton. That's where John Armstrong and the president are getting their information. Jonah was sure of that. Then, another question came to mind. Am I a decoy; openly sent by the president to be an encouraging force. Someone General Harrison could point a finger at, as taking news, when it was really Hampton or one of his cronies. No, he didn't think so. He had known Armstrong too long. Well, he couldn't worry about that now. He had to prepare himself for a duel. Still, he wouldn't completely dismiss it... not yet anyway.

The smell of fresh coffee greeted Jonah when he opened the cabin door. Moses was back and had obviously introduced himself to Anastasia. He could be charming when he wanted to. He had proved a good host as the two were drinking coffee and what was left of an unfinished pastry was in a plate sitting on the hearth. If Anastasia had been fearful of the half African, half Indian, it did not show at this point.

"There's coffee in the kitchen," Moses volunteered. "We saved you an apple turnover, as well."

"Thank you," Jonah replied.

As there were only two chairs, he sat on the edge of the bed hoping Moses would find some reason to vacate the cabin.

Finally, Jonah asked, "Did you find that cat?"

"Cat... what cat?"

"The cat Captain Todd almost stepped on last night. The one you said you wanted to see about this morning."

"I didn't go looking for a cat," Moses replied. "I went looking for firewood."

"Well, it doesn't look like you got enough."

"Enough? The box is running over now. It wouldn't hold another stick."

Damn you, Jonah thought. He then spotted the plate on the hearth. "Do you think the cook might need his plates back? It's getting on toward lunch."

A little giggle came from Anastasia.

Rising, Moses said, "Well, let me go see if I can find that cat and give it these scraps. I'll take these plates back to the cook so's he can add them to his stack of four or five hundred. While I'm at it, I will check his fire box and see if there's enough wood to cook the general's noon meal."

By this time, Anastasia was laughing so hard that tears came to her eyes. Jonah felt awkward and flushed but soon he was smiling as well.

"Would you like me to get your coffee and pastry?" Anastasia asked. "Then we can sit and talk if you'd like."

Before long, Jonah had learned Anastasia had been married for five years when her husband and his father had been killed by Indians. They had never had children. Her mother-in-law worked at the trading post until the British came and took everything that was worth taking. Food had been scarce. Two older officers had been billeted in her home. They had been nice, and their presence kept food on the table. Neither of them liked General Proctor, thinking him a coward and afraid of Tecumseh and his Indians. They did like Proctor's deputy, Lieutenant Colonel Warburton.

Warburton and his men had been ordered to destroy the town and everything in it when the Americans came.

"Only you got here sooner than expected," she said. "But don't think they've given up," she warned, her voice suddenly trembling with emotion. "Especially the Indians. One of the Indians said Tecumseh was spoiling for a fight. He'd even insulted Proctor trying to get him to attack. While the British may be retreating, Jonah, don't expect the Indians to give up easy. They'll fight and take scalps."

Her words caused Anastasia to shiver. Without thinking, Jonah placed his hands on hers. When she looked up, tears were in her eyes. He took out his handkerchief and handed it to her. Wiping her eyes, she said, "You be careful, Jonah. I don't want to see you hurt."

Chapter Twenty-One

THE PLACE WAS UNDER a large walnut tree not far from the river. The sun was on the western horizon and would be down in less than an hour. Jonah and LeRoche stood face to face, their blades in hand and pointed toward the ground. LeRoche had a rapier. It was a much smaller, slender blade with a fine point and a cutting edge. The blade was made for thrusting. Five men stood to the side under the large walnut tree... Five men and one woman. As hard as he tried, Jonah had not been able to talk Anastasia out of attending the duel. She now stood between Moses and Captain Hampton. A sixth man, a doctor, was also acting as referee. He was a portly, red-faced man with a huge nose.

As the two duelists stood toe to toe, the sight of his opponent almost caused Jonah to laugh. He was able to control the laughter but a smile broke out. LeRoche's nose was blue and swollen as was his left eye. Seeing the smirk on Jonah's face caused the man to clinch his teeth. His face grim, his eyes burned in rage at Jonah's behavior.

"Monsieur," he hissed with a French accent. "I will kill you."

"You will try," Jonah replied with more conviction than he really felt.

"Gentlemen... gentlemen," the physician referee spoke. "Insults are not needed. Is first blood sufficient to satisfy honor and end the contest?"

"It is not," LeRoche swore, the French accent was a shade more pronounced.

Jonah saw out of the corner of his eye that Anastasia clutched his handkerchief to her breasts. Moses looked stricken with fear. His long rifle standing at his side, firmly gripped in his right hand. *Right or wrong*, Jonah thought, *if I fall there will be a dead Frenchman as well.* The referee had been speaking, but as Jonah's mind had been wandering, he hadn't heard.

"Mr. Lee... I say, Mr. Lee!"

"Yes."

"If there are to be no apologies, are you ready to begin?"

"Yes."

"Then you may begin."

At this, LeRoche stepped back. He was elegantly dressed in a silken shirt, tight breeches, and a ruffled stock. Hampton had loaned Jonah a silk shirt.

"It is better if you are wounded," Hampton had advised. The shirt was a tight fit and was opened at the neck.

As LeRoche took a step back, he swished his blade back and forth in the air. Satisfied, he raised his rapier in salute with an elaborate gesture. Jonah returned the gesture with as much flourish as he could master. Suddenly, LeRoche leaped forward, his blade poised. Caught off balance, Jonah raised his blade just in time to deflect the initial thrust of his foe. Cruel eyes sparkled as LeRoche had all but ended the contest before it began.

Jonah's blade was a much heavier officer's sword. Single edged with a good hilt, there would be little clatter of blades. The rapier could not hold up against the army sword, therefore, LeRoche would do his best to inflect wounds without tying up blades in riposte. While Jonah's sword was superior in strength, it was also more awkward for this type of fight. It was made for cut and slash fighting, not a duel.

Realizing he would tire sooner than his adversary, Jonah decided to let LeRoche be the attacker, and he would, he hoped, parry the attack until such opportunity arose to end the duel or his foe grew tired. Then he would have the advantage... if only he could live so long.

Seeing Jonah had been caught off balance and surprised by his swift attack, LeRoche pressed his attack. He came forward with a fury causing Jonah to give ground. He parried three rapid cuts, and then felt a sting to his left side along the ribs.

Delighted, LeRoche giggled... almost a woman's giggle. "You will weaken now, m'sieur, as your blood flows, so will the knowledge that you will die this day."

"One of us will, Frenchman," Jonah retorted.

Angered, LeRoche attacked again. It was all Jonah could do as he parried several cuts trying desperately to fend off LeRoche's lightening-fast attack. A sudden thrust aimed at his throat was wide, causing LeRoche to lose balance. A backward slash connected and Jonah felt his sword bite into the Frenchman's flesh. LeRoche stepped back, clutching his left arm; blood now staining the white silk shirt. A look of alarm caused by the unorthodox maneuver replaced LeRoche's previous look of confidence. As the two men circled, Jonah was suddenly aware a crowd had gathered... was still gathering. *How had word gotten out*, he wondered.

The crowd had made a circle so that the two men fought in a ring made of humans. Moses now had Anastasia by the hand, the long rifle still firmly gripped in the other. LeRoche was more cautious now. During the next few minutes the men circled, feeling out each other's style.

While LeRoche was quick and agile, Jonah had excellent reflexes and a natural instinct, plus he was stronger. However, LeRoche's experience and enthusiasm for cruelty made him very dangerous. As the men circled, it dawned on LeRoche that his blade was longer by several inches. He now went on the attack again, yet keeping his distance away from Jonah's shorter blade. Intent on Jonah's death, every thrust was now aimed for the heart or throat.

After a parry knocked LeRoche's blade upward and caused a small cut to Jonah's face, the Frenchman seemed delighted again. "Your eyes may be next," he hissed.

LeRoche's comments angered Jonah and suddenly he went on the offensive. Disbelief that the American would do so caused LeRoche to back up until the crowd had to give way to keep from interfering in the fight. After a minute of cutting and slashing, Jonah got control of his anger and slowed his attack. Mistaking Jonah's let up was from fatigue rather than gaining control of his anger, the Frenchman drove forward. He slashed, cut, and thrust. As Jonah backed away, LeRoche threw caution to the wind and drove forward, all consumed by the desire to kill his foe. Nothing else mattered.

Jonah had watched his attacker and realized every time he made a thrust for his throat he'd plant his left foot then lurch forward. The two men warily circled each other. At some point, Jonah had been cut on the back of his hand but didn't feel it. Blood now oozed from the wound making the hilt of his sword slippery and sticky. Without meaning to, Jonah glanced down at the wound.

Taking advantage of the distraction, LeRoche lunged forward with vigor. The shift of the man's feet was just enough to warn Jonah. As LeRoche lunged for the throat, Jonah ducked down and with all his might thrust upward with his sword impaling his enemy. The blade went in just under the sternum. A look of dismay swept over LeRoche's face. Sure that victory was his; he looked down at the sword in his chest. As he fell backward, the slippery handle was jerked from Jonah's hand.

As his eyes glazed over, LeRoche spoke defiantly, "Tell the whore it was my Indians who killed her husband. His scalp lies in my drawer. Ha... hum.

Captain Hampton walked forward with the physician. "Please care for my friend's wound, Doctor, before he is attacked by ill humors." He then reached over and tried to pull the sword from the dead

Frenchman. As he pulled, the body lifted with the sword. Hampton then placed his foot on the dead man's chest and snatched the blade free. He wiped it on the dead man's britches then picked up the fallen rapier. He offered it to Jonah, who was still being tended to by the doctor.

"No, thank you," Jonah said. "It's yours if you desire it."

Hampton smiled, "A gift for my services." He then handed Jonah his sword. "I wiped it off, but I'd have it thoroughly cleaned before it was placed back in its scabbard."

"Thank you," Jonah said, wincing from the doctor's administrations.

Moses and Anastasia walked up from behind. Seeing them, Hampton said, "LeRoche was a double agent. Your killing him kept us from a hanging. We'll talk about it more later. You have visitors now."

Jonah held out his left hand as the right was being bandaged. "Thank you, James."

"My pleasure, sir." With that, Hampton walked away.

Two arms enveloped Jonah from behind. "Thank God you are alive. I was so worried." Anastasia hugged Jonah tightly, crushing her breasts against the back of his head.

Suddenly, his wounds didn't hurt anymore. Looking up as Moses stepped around the stool he was sitting on, Jonah said, "I saw you watching with the long rifle in your hand."

"He was a dead man," Moses said, by way of an answer. "One way or another, he was a dead man. He just didn't know it. The general was here... watching," Moses said. "Might be some explaining to do."

At that time, Anastasia leaned forward again, kissing the cut on Jonah's face. *Explain to the general,* he thought. *Well, I will...later; much later.*

Chapter Twenty-Two

THE GENERAL HELD OFFICER'S call that evening at his headquarters. There was more than enough food and wine to sate everyone's appetite and thirst. Jonah seemed to have gained a degree of respect from some of the officers who thus far had known him as Armstrong's man or the president's man. Hampton had smoothed the way with the general by painting LeRoche not only as a traitor but a rapist.

Colonel Mentor Johnson was also on Jonah's side, adding to his daring do, by pointing out Jonah's bravery during several clashes with the Indians.

"If I didn't know better, I'd swear that 'un was from Kaintuck," Governor Shelby commented. For him, this was high praise, indeed.

Several toasts were drunk before General Harrison finally called the officers to attention. Without a specific plan of action laid out, he stated they would move out the following morning at daybreak. When asked about the lack of a specific battle plan, the general replied in a testy manner, "You have to catch the enemy before you lay out a plan of battle, Colonel. Once we are close, we will send out a reconnaissance and then make our plans accordingly."

Jonah didn't know the colonel personally but felt sorry for the man who had been brave or foolish enough, whichever the case may be, to ask what everyone else wanted to ask. It was by accident that Jonah picked up a slight nod by Edmond Gaines, the adjutant general. Following his gaze, Jonah realized the colonel must be one of Gaines' officers.

Gaines had made a name for himself at the Battle of Cryslers Farm. He was a man of distinction and would brook little abuse of one of his officers regardless of who it was from. He had been one of the first to congratulate Jonah on such a gallant display of swordsmanship.

With the only significant information being they'd march at sunrise, Jonah quickly tired of the small talk and waited until the general was distracted. He then slipped out a side door. As he made his way down the hall toward the back porch, he was called by Hampton.

"I would have thought you'd be having your wounds tended by some dark-haired beauty rather than listening to a bunch of old windbags."

This caused Jonah to chuckle, but he couldn't help but glance about to make sure some of those 'old windbags' hadn't heard. Smiling, Jonah again thanked Hampton for all his support. The two men shook hands and then said goodnight.

As Jonah entered the cabin, Moses was propped back in a chair eating a chicken leg. One he'd stolen from the general's kitchen, no doubt. Jonah then noted two bottles of wine sitting on the little table.

Moses rocked his chair forward and stood up, "Took you long enough."

"Why do you say that?" Jonah asked.

Moses rolled his eyes but didn't speak. He picked up the bottle of wine that was still corked, grabbed his long rifle and said, "Come on. I've already got the horses saddled." Neither spoke as they headed down the street.

"Where are we going?" Jonah asked finally.

"Don't try to be coy with me, Jonah. You know where we are going. I wouldn't doubt that young lady ain't already in bed by now, though."

"Why are you going?" Jonah inquired, excited by the prospect of seeing Anastasia but not wanting any company.

"Don't worry," Moses muttered. "I won't interfere with your sparkin' none. I'm just going to sit outside and make sure no one else interferes."

"Thank you, my friend," Jonah said, putting his hand on Moses' arm as they rode on.

The door was quickly answered when Jonah knocked. "I've been wondering when you'd come," Anastasia said softly as she closed the door. She sat the bottle of wine on a table. As she turned, Jonah could see she wore a lavender gown, cut low in the front so that a goodly portion of cleavage was visible; the sight was breathtaking.

Jonah followed her into a small sitting room. Anastasia sat on a couch and patted the space next to her indicating where Jonah was to sit. Her elbows at her side and her hands in her lap, Anastasia looked at Jonah's eyes. Deep into his eyes so that she seemed to peer right through into his very soul. Reaching over, Jonah took hold of her arm and pulled her to him. She responded with unashamed passion and they clung together. Her breasts were pushing into his chest, their mouths as one in a long, enduring kiss that had them both gasping for breath.

Jonah had been without a woman for many months, and the passionate kiss roused him almost beyond control. Anastasia had him almost to the edge of his control. Each caress, each kiss more insatiable and demanding than the one before. Jonah reached to undo her dress.

Anastasia broke free and said, "Not here." She took his hand and led him into her bedroom.

A small candle flickered on the table by her bed. Jonah sat on the edge of the bed and reached out but Anastasia pulled away. Slowly, she loosened a ribbon in her hair. Shaking her head, she let it fall down over her shoulder. Then, in the dim candlelight, she removed the string at her waist and the gown fell open revealing the most perfect breasts Jonah had ever seen. So intent was he at her chest, he failed to note the gown had slid to the floor until the woman was up close again.

Slowly, she removed his shirt, boots, and britches. The last barrier was down now. All reserve wiped away by the need two people had for one another. Later, the war and even the world seemed so remote. Somewhere in the distance, the rumble of thunder was heard causing Anastasia to snuggle closer. Spent from his passion, Jonah relaxed. He was more at peace than he had been in some time. As he absently curled a lock of Anastasia's hair, he felt content for the first time in a long time. Another rumble was heard, closer this time.

Easing up on his elbow pulled at Jonah's wound, causing him to wince. Anastasia pressed her bare flesh to his chest and kissed each of his wounds, the wetness of a tear dropping on his skin.

"You've suffered. For me, you risk your life." Her lips found his again. Salty tasting kisses as a result of her tears, but still warm, loving, and passionate.

As minutes melted into an hour, Jonah whispered, "I have to get up."

"I know, it's just I don't want this night to end."

"I feel the same."

As they sat up, Anastasia looked at Jonah and said, "You leave tomorrow."

He nodded and then added, "At first light."

Watching Jonah dress, Anastasia propped herself up but didn't cover herself. Sitting on the edge of the bed to put on his boots, Jonah cocked his head and said, "You're not making it easy for me."

"I don't want it to be." Jonah smiled at this. Then, in a quivering, trembling voice, she continued, "After tonight, what do I do with my life?"

Her words seem to tear the heart out of his chest as he leaned over and they embraced.

"Have you thought of moving south?" he asked.

Surprise swept over her face. Jonah was even surprised he asked it… but didn't regret it.

Before he could change his mind, Jonah continued, "The general will leave a company of soldiers here until we return. That shouldn't be too long… a week, two at the most. You be ready when I return."

A sudden bounce and a nude Anastasia was in his arms. "You mean it, don't you? Jonah, you really mean it?"

"Of course I do," he said, as he popped her bare bottom. "Now get to bed and dream sweet dreams while I round up Moses and get back to headquarters before it rains again."

Smiling, Anastasia stood and on tip-toes wrapped her arms around her man and gave him another long kiss, crushing her body into his rough clothing. "I love you," she whispered.

"And I you," Jonah replied, thinking *how many times have I said that, but this time I think I mean it.*

Stepping outside, the air had a nip in it, and there was a breeze blowing. It hadn't started to rain yet, but you could smell it in the air. Moses was sitting on a rail fence surrounding a small lean-to. Someone had built it for a horse, mule, or maybe even a milk cow. It was all but down now. Something a man could fix but a chore not likely undertaken by a woman… not without help.

"Sorry to take so long," Jonah apologized to his friend.

"You needed it," Moses replied. "Didn't deserve it," he joked, "but you needed it."

"Hush, you old scoundrel," Jonah hissed.

Both men were smiling as they rode to the camp. A soldier, standing guard at the entrance of the headquarters, waved as the two men rode around the corner of the house to the backyard, stable, and their cabin.

Once the horses were cared for, Moses built a fire in the cabin's small fireplace. He reached for the bottle of wine and asked about a glass before bed.

"Might as well, we never opened the other bottle," Jonah replied. "Oh well, something for her to remember me by."

"You," Moses snorted. "I'm the one who took it."

Chapter Twenty-Three

A KNOCK AT THE DOOR surprised Jonah and Moses. It was Clay Gesslin and James Hampton. Moses let them in and offered what was left of the wine.

"No thanks," Hampton said, declining the wine. It was obvious he had important news. "We have just had one of my men return with news of Proctor," he said, getting right to the point. "My man says Proctor was fit to be tied after hearing Perry defeated Barclay. In fact, his words were..." Hampton paused, as he pulled a paper from his coat, unfolded it and read, "*The loss of the fleet is a most calamitous circumstance. I do not see the least chance of occupying to advantage my present position, which can be so easily turned by means of the entire command of the waters here which the enemy now has, a circumstance that would render my Indian force very inefficient. It is my opinion that I should retire on the Thames without delay...*"

"So it's to be the Thames," Jonah said excited.

"That it is. General Harrison plans to march at daybreak, only now we have a destination."

"What about the militia?" Jonah asked.

They had balked when Hull had wanted to push on into Canada. After the River Raisin massacre the militia was now ready to ride to hell and back if need be to get revenge for the brutal way their comrades had been slaughtered after surrendering to the British.

The early morning light was creeping over the horizon. The clouds were gray and would remain so as a light drizzle fell. The smell of charred wood drifted on the air from across the river where in Detroit the British had burned down two hundred or so buildings.

General Harrison in his rain-soaked uniform was at the head of the column. He motioned for Jonah to join him as they rode into the dreary day. He suddenly seemed a different man.

"Well, Jonah, we finally know where the enemy is so we march to victory or death. Does that not stir your soul?"

"Hopefully, it will be victory without the latter," Jonah answered with a smile.

"Quite right, my man."

Keeping with the precedent he had established by leaving a brigade behind to garrison Detroit and Fort Malden, Harrison did the same at Sandwich. The garrison was left under the command of Lewis Cass, who spit and spewed about being left behind but to no avail.

Jonah quietly took Cass aside and asked if he would keep his eye on Anastasia for him. With LeRoche dead, she should be safe but one never knew.

With a grin spreading across his face, Cass replied, "I will be glad to keep my eye on her."

Jonah thanked him and started to go but wheeled around, catching the hidden meaning behind Cass' words. "Keep your eye on her, huh," Jonah said.

Cass chuckled in spite of himself. "Don't worry, Jonah, we will keep her safe for you."

Commodore Perry had sailed the *Ariel* and *Caledonia* as close to the shore as he dared. His ships could go no further. However, determined not to be left out of the overland pursuit of the British, he had borrowed a white horse and now rode on General Harrison's right.

After an hour's march, the land started to change. Colonel Johnson rode forward and recommended his mounted rifles take the point. The general accepted the recommendation with a mere nod.

Wheeling his horse around, the colonel asked, "Care to join us, Mr. Lee.?"

Hesitating, Jonah turned to General Harrison. He did not want to insult the general after being invited to ride beside him. Finally, the urge was too strong.

"With your permission, General," he said.

"Go ahead, Jonah, onward to glory."

"Thank you, sir." Jonah waited till Johnson's mounted rifles were abreast, and then with a wave to the general, fell in beside Captain Gesslin and galloped off.

The mounted rifles tore through the sodden countryside, their horses splashing muddy water from potholes. The infantry had a much more difficult time of it trying to pass through the quagmire left behind by the mounted rifles horses. The rain that had begun to fall on the day Harrison's forces occupied Sandwich, continued to fall off and on.

"At least we won't die of thirst," Major David Thompson volunteered to Jonah.

"Might get a bit chilly, though," Jonah replied as he tugged at his sodden clothes.

It was proving to be a hard march. The army followed the river road toward Saint Claire. Moses eased up beside Jonah and said, "You see all these deserted farms?" Jonah nodded. Moses continued, "Fine looking farms, all deserted due to this war. Crops wasting, cows running about, and people's lives ruined. It's sad," he said, shaking his head.

Jonah nodded again, his thoughts back with the woman he'd just left.

Recognizing Jonah's mind was elsewhere, Moses said, "You better get your mind off that girl until this here fighting is over. There'll be time enough for you to go mooning after we whip the Redcoats."

These comments did bring a smile to Jonah, but still he didn't speak. The two had been together long enough for Moses to know it would do no good to push.

Johnson's mounted rifles reached Saint Claire and set up a perimeter.

"This will be as good a place as any for the infantry to take a breather," Lieutenant Colonel James Johnson spoke to his sons, Edward and William.

They went to their horses and returned with a coffee pot, coffee, and some dry kindling. *If they get a fire going, the hot coffee would be invigorating,* Jonah thought. Seeing what the boys were at, Moses dismounted and took the two boys in tow directing them to a deserted shed. It had a stoop where the pole on the right had rotted and fallen away so that it canted significantly.

"We could prop up that side," Edward volunteered.

"We might," Moses agreed, "then again that could bring the whole blasted thing down on our ears. It'll give us shelter enough to get a fire going and the coffee boiling. If we are to tarry after we have our coffee, then we can try shoring it up a bit."

The two boys agreed, with William saying, "Couldn't get but three or four under there even if it was fixed up."

The men rested and drank their coffee along with what spirits had been smuggled to aid against the rain and cold. Mounting his horse, Colonel Mentor Johnson moaned "Damnable weather has me aching all over."

"Me as well," his brother added.

Hearing a noise, the group turned to see General Harrison's infantry arriving. The roads were nothing but ruts of mud, but still they had made good time.

"We left the fires banked for you, General," Johnson volunteered as he saluted Harrison.

Nodding, Harrison thanked the colonel and ordered a rest as he dismounted. Thinking of his time aboard ship with the commodore, Jonah greeted Perry.

"That horse is a might tougher on the bottom than a ship's quarter-deck, isn't it, Commodore?"

Smiling, Perry dismounted and pulled at his sodden trousers. "Well, you won't get saddle sores on board ship and that's no error."

"Huh..." Jonah mused. "So we are not likely to see you resign your naval commission and join the army?" This brought a chuckle from the group.

Perry eyed Jonah and smiling said, "Touché."

"With your leave, General, we'll resume our forward position," Colonel Johnson said, itching to be moving along. Harrison nodded and saluted but didn't speak. Wheeling his horse, the colonel spoke to his officers, "Move 'em out, gentlemen."

For the next several miles the country grew more barren and less settled, with marshes stretching as far as one could see. The mounted rifles had only ridden for half an hour when Sergeant Wilcox, who was with the detail riding point, galloped up.

"Captain Sympson's compliments, sir. We appear to be catching up with stragglers from the British column."

This was good news indeed. Speaking to his brother, he said, "Send William back to the general with my dispatch."

Colonel Mentor Johnson's secretary, Major W.T. Barry, held his cloak and hat over the pad on which the colonel scribbled a quick note. Folding the note, he handed it to his brother's youngest son. "Get this to the general as fast as you can, William, but don't kill your horse getting there."

"Yes sir," the boy replied, excited that he was being trusted with such an important errand but nervous about going alone.

Seeing the boy's conflict of emotion, Moses spoke, "If the colonel doesn't mind, I'll ride back with the boy and keep him company."

Relief flooded the boy's face, but Moses didn't miss the nod and thank you Lieutenant Colonel James Johnson mouthed.

As the two men spurred their horses away, Colonel Mentor Johnson spoke again, "Let's close with the point. Be ready with your weapons but don't cock them. I don't want to lose anybody from some accident."

Chapter Twenty-Four

COLONEL JOHNSON SET A fast pace, determined to catch up with the stragglers before they knew something was amiss. He knew his point riders would give nothing away unless by chance they were spotted or attacked. Jonah couldn't help but wonder if the colonel wasn't trying to build on his war hawk reputation and show his willingness to bring the enemy to battle ahead of General Harrison's arrival. Such a bold move could do nothing but bolster his political ambition and position. Major David Thompson was waiting on Johnson at the rear of his point guard. When Johnson spotted him, he held up his hand and the mounted rifles slowed to a walk.

"What do we have Major?" Johnson asked, getting right to the point.

"Rear guard most likely, sir. Wagons loaded down, a few Redcoats and Indians, along with a lot of women and children. Captain Sympson is trailing the group now, sir."

"Is there a clear separation or are they all scattered about?"

"Scattered about mostly, sir."

"Hmmph," Johnson sighed. This put an end to his thoughts of a quick charge with sabers rattling and guns blasting, A bunch of dead women and children would not help his political future at all. Butcher was not a name he could hope to succeed with. Turning to his aid, he ordered, "Pass the word for Captain Gesslin."

"I'm here, sir."

"Good," Johnson replied. "Clay," he said, using Gesslin's first name, "I want you to take your company and swing around the edge of the marsh and see if you can't get ahead of the British. When you are in position, let go with three shots one right after the other. That will be our signal to close. If you are sighted, go ahead and give the alarm. We'll just have to do the best we can not to harm any woman or child."

The officer muttered his understanding and Jonah fell in beside Gesslin as the men rode off. Trying to keep out of sight and at the same time keep from getting bogged down along the edge of the marshy area proved trying. However, the steady downpour of rain helped. Several times Jonah thought they'd been seen but the buckskins most of the riders wore blended in with the woods better than Jonah could have hoped for.

Most of the British column was on foot but even the few driving the wagons or those on horseback had their collars pulled up and their hats pulled down against the element.

At one point, Gesslin sidled up to Jonah and chanced a whispered comment. "That's a beaten lot if ever I saw one. Look at how they drag their feet. Not an ounce of life in the whole bunch." Nodding, Jonah agreed.

By the time they got ahead of the group, they had already passed four wagons. One appeared to be loaded down with sick or wounded men. The other three had supplies loaded in them and the last wagon was also pulling a small cannon.

"Probably a six-pounder," Jonah guessed.

Women, both Indian and white, along with children walked behind the wagons. The odd Indian brave rode with the group. There were twenty riders, including Indians and Redcoats. A sergeant, who Gesslin had sent ahead, was waiting as the rest of the company rode into the road.

"There's a bend just yonder," the sergeant said, pointing. "Past that there's maybe three or four hundred yards of a narrow straight-away with thick woods and marsh on either side. We could ride ahead to the end of the straight, and when they get passed the bend, fire off the alarm. The folk might scatter, but those wagons ain't going nowhere with the marsh on each side."

"Good idea, Hicks," Gesslin replied, agreeing with the man's plans. He deployed his men on either side of the road hoping they'd blend in with the forest until it was too late for the British to do much. Nervous horses pawed the wet ground. The Kentuckians had all checked their rifles, and the flints and priming pans were covered with coats and hats as the rain continued.

The sound of jingling trace chains were soon heard as the first wagon rounded the bend. Beside and behind the wagon, the first riders were seen slouched over and obviously miserable. The second wagon rounded the bend and at the same time one of the Kentuckian's horses whinnied. Heads of the Indian and British riders jerked up, suddenly alert.

"That does it," Gesslin hissed, then shouted his order to fire.

What followed was not what had been planned. Upon the word fire, the Kentuckians, instead of firing off three shots in the air, fired at the riders emptying six saddles with the volley. The other horsemen tried to calm their animals as those whose rider had been shot wheeled around in a wild panic. One rider was thrown and hit the muddy ground with a thud, splashing muddy water as he landed. Some of the riders in the rear wheeled and headed back down the trial while a handful, mostly Indians charged at Gesslin's men.

Jonah had not fired his long rifle but as the Indians charged, he picked out a target and pulled the trigger. The damp powder flashed but not enough to fire his ball. By the time, Jonah realized he had a misfire; the Indian was almost on him. Dropping the rifle to the ground, Jonah quickly drew his sword all the time dreading the cleaning job that would have to be done on his fine weapon. The charging Indian was whooping and hollering, shaking a tomahawk in the air. The Indian let loose with the weapon, when the two men were no more than eight feet apart.

Jonah almost fell from the saddle as he ducked, the tomahawk making a whooshing sound as it swept past his ear. He'd just regained his balance when the Indian brave was upon him. Instead of galloping off toward freedom, the Indian collided into Jonah's horse and the two toppled to the muddy ground. The Indian's momentum carried him over Jonah, landing several feet away. The Indian pulled his knife from its scabbard and charged. Jonah had not had time to put his sword's lanyard around his wrist and the collision with the Indian had knocked it from his grip.

Seeing the Indian up with his knife, Jonah frantically felt the muddy ground about him. He felt the blade and realizing he was on top of the hilt, rolled over to get a hold of the sword. The rolling man made the horse jump about, hooves stomping the ground almost at Jonah's head. The jumping horse saved Jonah's life as it swung around, its hindquarters knocked the Indian sprawling into the mud. Now, Jonah was on his feet with sword in his hand. As Jonah approached, the Indian now looked for his weapon which had been jarred loose when the horse tumbled him. Whether it was bad luck for the Indian or good luck for Jonah, the brave gave up his search for the lost knife.

Jumping to his feet, the Indian gave Jonah a cold look, spat mud from his mouth and then turned, dashing off into the marsh. Heaving a deep sigh, Jonah wiped the muddy grit from his face, lifting it skyward so that the rain would help clean his face.

In the distance, the sound of sporadic rifle fire was heard. Gesslin's men had spread out, and the wagon drivers were standing with their hands up. Spotting his rifle lying in the mud, Jonah picked it up and looking down the barrel, it seemed clear. However, it would have to be thoroughly cleaned before it was fired.

"Decide to play in the mud, did you?" Clay Gesslin said, as he rode up.

"Not so's you'd notice," Jonah snarled.

"Well, if you're through," Gesslin continued, ignoring Jonah's reply. "You can mount up and we can see what plunder we've taken."

Jonah mounted and saw Colonel Johnson and General Harrison's group looking at the wagons. The general must have ridden ahead of the infantry, Jonah decided. Moses rode up taking in Jonah's appearance but not saying anything.

"Anybody hurt?" Jonah asked.

"None of ours. A few British, but when they saw us, most of them just threw up their hands."

"What about the women and children?"

A grin came to Moses' face. "They're fine. As soon as we rode up, this woman says, 'Well, Gov'nor, took you long enough. Got any food?' The general appeared a little flustered by the woman's approach. Nevertheless, he says, 'I'm sure we can find something, Madame'. The woman then says, 'Lord love you, doll, and if you be needing a little company later just send word and Maggie will be right over to his lordship's tent to give comfort.' This caused the other generals and the commodore to laugh but Harrison grunts and says, 'I'm sure that won't be necessary.' Determined to have the final say, the woman says, 'Well, if you does, just remember it's Maggie'."

Chapter Twenty-Five

B Y SUNDOWN, THE RAIN had ceased and Johnson's mounted rifles had reached the mouth of the Thames River. The river was high from all the rain and flowing swiftly. Here, the land opened up to a large prairie. The narrow road with marshes was behind them.

Looking at the extensive opening, Colonel Johnson addressed Jonah, "A pretty land, is it not, Mr. Lee?"

"Yes, sir. That it is."

"Good farm land," Johnson continued, "good pasture land as well. Cows, horses, and mules, good graze for all of them." Then, speaking to everyone, he announced, "We'll camp here tonight. There is plenty of room for us and the general's group when they get here. Reckon we'll have time to inventory the plunder."

Jonah didn't say anything, but he'd bet there'd already been an unofficial inventory and anything worth taking, other than military supplies, had already been confiscated. As the word was passed, men began to unsaddle and rub down the weary horses. Then, in small groups, they were taken down to the river and watered. One area next to a line of hickory trees still had a stand of grass growing that had not been killed by the early morning frost.

"Those trees kept most of the frost away," Moses volunteered.

The horses were hobbled and let loose to graze. Several men were assigned to picket the area. Once the horses were cared for, the men began to collect firewood and brush for their bedrolls to lie atop of. The fires were lit and going good by the time General Harrison's main body arrived.

Several men had rigged fishing poles and were pulling in fish almost as quick at they threw out their lines. Seeing the fish lying on the bank, the captive women began picking them up and cleaning them. Soon, frying pans were sizzling with lard and were ready for the fish to be fried. After the fish were cooked, a batter of corn meal was mixed up and a spoon at a time dropped into the sizzling grease. Almost as soon as the batter was dropped, it sunk to the bottom of the pan and then floated to the top. The women expertly tipped the corn dodgers, flipping them over and then in a minute or less, picked up a crispy, tasty corn dodger from the boiling grease.

"I've had a lot of fish before," General Harrison volunteered, "but nothing this tasty."

Seeing the commodore wiping his hands on his pants leg, Jonah said, "Is this as good as what you are accustomed to, Commodore?"

Taking a sip of coffee, Perry wiped his mouth with the back of his hand, and then after a small belch replied, "You may find this amazing, Mr. Lee, but it's a rare occasion when we poor sailors eat fish. I don't know the reason for it, but there seems to be an aversion to them."

This did surprise Jonah, but before he could discuss the matter further, a lieutenant from the infantry walked up and requested to speak to the general. While there were several gathered around, everyone knew he was talking about Harrison.

Hearing the request, Harrison called out, "Bring the man forward, sir."

The officer left then quickly returned. As the lieutenant came closer to the fire, one of the British prisoners was with him. The lieutenant came to attention and quickly came to the point. "Sir, this is Sergeant Calloway. He is the senior British soldier. He wants to know if they are to be offered parole."

"Parole," Harrison repeated.

"Yes sir."

"Do you trust him, Lieutenant...?"

"Anderson, Lieutenant Anderson, from Ohio."

"Yes, well, thank you for your service, Lieutenant. Now, do you trust the man to speak for all the British?"

"Yes sir, I do. I think they were moving slowly expecting to be overtaken."

"I see," Harrison said, and then gave his attention to the sergeant. "If I take your parole, Sergeant, can you guarantee your soldiers will abide by it?"

"Yes, your Lordship. My soldiers and the women will abide by it. I can't speak for the Indians."

"You may address me as General Harrison. We have no lords in this army."

"Yes sir."

"Now tell me, Sergeant, why can't you speak for the Indians?"

"Well, your Lord... I mean, General, they ain't under my command. They seem to come and go as they please; the braves that is. They mostly come when it's time to eat. They will fight iffen they's fightin' to do. I don't 'magine they'd know or understand the meaning of parole. Iffen it was me, your Lordship... General, I'd post an extra guard on the horses and let 'em slip away tonight. Otherwise, they'll be more trouble than they're worth. Course, as well as you fed 'em they may decide they like being took and hang around. It's been a time since we have eaten this good."

"Yes well, I'll take your word of honor as to parole. Your women have already proved their worth with this fine meal."

"Thank you, sir, and they are mighty comforting on cool nights, too."

This caused Harrison to flush and Commodore Perry to chuckle.

"Yes, Sergeant, but I don't think that will be necessary," Harrison replied. "Now your word, Sergeant."

"You have my word, my Lord...er, General."

Harrison thanked the sergeant and then dismissed him. He called to his adjutant. "Make sure to double the guard on the horses and ere, Major, pass the word I'll discipline any man fighting with the British soldiers or otherwise engaged with the captive women."

"Yes sir."

"Major, before you go, do you have the inventory from the wagons?"

"Yes sir. There were ten cases of muskets, twelve barrels of gun-powder, a case of flints, the six-pounder as you saw but no shot for it. There was no food and nothing else of military significance."

"I see, Major, but exactly what do you mean of military significance?"

The general has put the major on the spot, Jonah thought. He knows the men have pilfered the wagons but doesn't want to tell.

"I think what the major means, General, is the rest were personal belongings that the captives had. Cooking materials and stuff," Jonah volunteered. This brought him two different looks; one of annoyance from Harrison while a look of gratitude filled the major's face.

"Is that what you mean, Major?"

"Yes sir."

"Well, dammit man, say so. Don't depend on the man from Washington to do your talking."

Jonah felt the sting from Harrison's barbed words and started to reply but knew it would only make it worse for the major.

"I think Mr. Lee spoke from personal knowledge," Colonel Johnson volunteered. "Being at the point, we had the opportunity to observe the wagons prior to the main body's arrival."

Jonah was thankful of the colonel coming to his defense. He also noted two things: the colonel said observe, not inspect. Therefore, his statement had not been a lie. Also, he hadn't missed the opportunity to drive home it was his men who were first on the scene. The general grunted something that Jonah couldn't make out, but the group broke up and the generals went to their respective tents.

When Jonah got back to his campsite Moses was drinking coffee. He poured a cup for Jonah, handed it to him, and picked up his friend's long rifle. He oiled the weapon and then took a rag and wiped the excess oil from it.

"You did a good job cleaning the mud off," Moses said.

"I had some gun oil and felt a light coat might help. Thank you," Jonah said absently; his mind on Harrison once more.

Was his presence and the knowledge he was from Washington any help? Colonel Johnson had commented how he appreciated Jonah being there, as now he had someone to help motivate the general to seek out the British.

"I don't know that I've been much of a motivating force," Jonah had replied.

"Sure you have, sir, otherwise we would still be at Camp Seneca."

Jonah had taken solace in the colonel's words. I must be a thorn in the general's side, he decided. Not sure he liked the role, but if it would help win the war, he was glad to do it. Moses, Jonah realized, was packing a small sack and had his bedroll under his arm.

"Where are you going?"

Moses smiled then replied, "There's a lot more squaws out there than there is braves. One or two have expressed the desire to have someone watch over them and protect them from these heathen Kentuckians."

Nodding his head in understanding, Jonah said, "I'm sure you have offered your services as protector for the remainder of our travels."

"As I should," Moses answered.

"Well, be careful, the general has promised to discipline any soldier getting in trouble over the women."

"There will be no trouble," Moses said. "Besides I ain't no soldier. I'm the scout for the president's man."

This caused Jonah to laugh. "Well, there's that."

Moses had no sooner disappeared than Clay Gesslin and James Hampton walked up. Hampton dropped a bottle in Jonah's lap before he could speak.

"Major Martin's compliments."

Picking up the bottle, Jonah said, "This is French wine."

"That it is," Hampton agreed. "Part of them non-military stores that were confiscated. Now, pop the cork so we can enjoy it, else we'll take it to the general's tent."

A 'pop' echoed above the crackle of the fire, and the men filled their cups.

Chapter Twenty-Six

THE SKY WAS FULL of ragged clouds, and there was still a bright moon as Harrison's army rolled out of their blankets. Men walked into the shadows to answer nature's call. One or two fires still had small flames that flickered about, but most had died down to embers. As the embers were stirred, small firefly-like sparks drifted up toward the night sky. More firewood was added and soon the landscape was dotted with fires.

Jonah rose from his blankets. Moses had not returned during the night, but he'd likely show up soon. Hampton was curled up next to the remnants of their fire but Gesslin was nowhere to be seen. *Probably rousted out by his sergeant*, Jonah thought.

Bumping Hampton's legs with his foot, Jonah called to his friend. "Get up and piss, the world's on fire."

"Let it burn," Hampton growled.

Jonah walked off to relieve himself; when he returned Hampton was sitting up. "Damn sorry way to treat a guest at your fire," Hampton muttered as he fed twigs into the embers. Somebody could be heard approaching, and both men turned toward the noise.

"Damned if you couldn't sneak up on a body if you were a mind to," Hampton said to Moses as he became visible.

"If I was a mind to, your hair would be hanging from my long rifle," Moses said with a smile. He then removed a sack from his shoulders and laid out leftover corn dodgers and bacon. He picked the coffee pot up that had gotten knocked over during the night and filled it with water from a canteen, and then, setting it on the fire, got water boiling for coffee to be made.

"Did you keep watch over our captives?" Jonah asked.

"Two of them I did," Moses replied matter-of-factly. "I could have watched over more, but I didn't want to appear hoggish to our Kentucky friends." This caused Hampton and Jonah to chuckle.

"This bacon is still warm," Jonah volunteered.

"Course it is so are the corn dodgers," Moses answered. Once the water was hot, Moses added grounds.

Seeing Hampton watching, Jonah explained, "Moses likes to boil the water before adding coffee, says it improves the taste."

"Does it?" Hampton asked.

"Well, anything is an improvement over my coffee, but yeah, I think it does."

"I'm ready to try it out," Hampton said, smacking as he did so. "Anything is better than this taste I've got right now."

"Too much wine," Moses said, and then looking down and seeing a cigar butt, added, "And tobacco."

After breakfast Hampton stood, belched and said, "I better go check in with the chaplain."

By that, he meant Major James Sugget. Officially, he was head of the scouts. Jonah was certain the word 'spies' could have been used just as well. Moses had retrieved their horses, and he and Jonah were packing up when Gesslin rode up.

"The colonel is sending us out to ride point; said to see if you want to come along. It appears the general is achy with his rheumatism and is in a foul mood."

Smiling, Jonah said, "I ought to hang back just to ruin his day, but that'd ruin mine as well. Give us a minute and we'll be ready."

As the point riders rode out, the sun came up, but it was late morning before the nip was out of the air. Another group of British stragglers were seen. These men were half-starved. Seeing the Americans, the soldiers laid down their weapons and held up their hands.

The first question asked when Gesslin rode up was, "You got any rations, yer Lordship?"

Feeling sorry for the ragged, half-starved soldiers, the Kentuckians pulled out what they had only to see it disappear immediately as the men wolfed it down.

"Hicks," Gesslin called to one of his men.

"Yes sir."

"March these men back to the main group."

"Yes sir!"

"Ere... yer Lordship!" The apparent leader of the group was speaking again.

"Yes."

Holding up his worn out boots and bloody ankles for Gesslin to see, the man asked, "Couldn't we just wait right here, sir? We done surrendered like and, of course, we'd give our parole. Besides, the man could be thar and back quicker without us holding him up."

Several men laughed causing Gesslin to turn quickly and stare. Then, unable to control himself, started laughing also. "All right," he said. "Find you a comfortable spot and light." He then looked at the British soldier who'd been talking and asked, "You're not a lawyer, are you?"

"No suh!" The reply was quick. "I'm a McAllister, sir... Sergeant McAllister."

This caused the men to laugh so hard one of the Kentuckians fell off his horse. Gesslin didn't even try to hide his laughter this time.

"What's so funny?" McAllister asked, causing the men to laugh more.

"I'm sorry, Sergeant," Gesslin managed. "Just good ole American humor."

"I see, sir. Uh, sir?"

"Yes, Sergeant."

"Would you mind if we fire off a musket?"

The sergeant's comment wiped the smile off Gesslin's face, suddenly alert to possible trickery. Seeing he'd created a touchy position for himself and his comrades, the sergeant quickly added, "It wouldn't go down good for us, sir, if it was found out we gave up without firing a shot."

"I see," Gesslin replied. "Hand me your weapon, Sergeant."

The man did as he was ordered. "It ain't loaded, sir," he said, handing up the weapon.

Gesslin expertly loaded and primed the weapon but left out the ball.

"Fire away, Sergeant."

The sergeant did so and thanked Gesslin. The men seemed relax again, and the sergeant sided up to Gesslin and whispered.

"You're certain?" Gesslin asked.

"That I am, sir."

"Hicks," Gesslin called again.

"Yes sir."

"I want you to take this dispatch to Colonel Johnson."

"Yes sir."

"Hicks."

"Yes sir."

"Ride like your feet is on fire and your arse is catching."

"Yes sir!"

Jonah watched as the rider galloped away. Gesslin then motioned to Jonah, and the two walked over to a clump of oak trees.

"That sergeant says the British have a couple of barges and a store house full of weapons not twenty miles from here at a place called McGregors Creek. He says there's not much of a guard there to keep us from taking them. Fact is he says they've been ordered to destroy everything when we are spotted and retreat."

"Why did he tell you?" Jonah asked, very suspicious of this news.

"He said he wouldn't have if we hadn't been so gentlemanly about the surrender. However, he feels Proctor has turned coward, and he doesn't trust the Red Devils as he put it. He figures as soon as this war is over he can go home."

"Do you trust him?" Jonah inquired, still suspicious.

"I'm not sure. I'd like to believe it, but I mentioned the colonel may want Captain Hampton to talk to the man before we go high-tailing it into some trap."

Jonah winced when Gesslin said the colonel and not the general. However, Johnson was Gesslin's reporting officer. It would be up to Johnson to make Harrison aware of the information.

"Riders coming, sir."

Gesslin and Jonah stood up from where they'd been resting. Pickets had been deployed so there was little concern of a surprise attack. The British soldiers had been enamored with Moses. The group had kept a conversation going while they waited on Hicks to return with orders or for the others to catch up. Standing, Jonah was able to make out General Harrison and Commodore Perry riding in the lead of Colonel Johnson's mounted rifles. This was a relief to Jonah, though he couldn't have explained why other than it was the way it should be. Johnson had proved a good soldier and hadn't let politics sway his decision.

As the group rode up, Jonah heard the general speaking to Hampton, "As soon as you get a good feel, Captain, let me know."

The man saluted and then dismounted, walked over to Gesslin, and the two talked in a low voice.

"Mr. Lee, I see you're feeling fit today."

"Yes sir. I had a good night's sleep."

"As you should," the general replied.

Damn, Jonah thought. *Does the old boy know about the wine?*

Chapter Twenty-Seven

CAPTAIN HAMPTON TALKED WITH each of the men, alone and then as a group. After the better part of an hour, he reported to the general he felt the men were truthful and that there was a good chance of capturing a significant amount of arms and men if they moved quickly. That meant the mounted rifles, as the slower infantry could never cover the distance before the sun went down.

"Ahem!" General Harrison and the other officers looked toward Jonah.

"Yes, Mr. Lee, you wish to add to the discussion?"

"Yes sir, if I may. The British at McGregors Creek have no idea when or even if we are coming. If we arrive in force after dark, it will be too late to adequately reconnoiter the area. Not only that, but an army bedding down for the night will alarm the British, who will destroy the supplies before we even get close." Jonah could see he held the officer's attention and some were even nodding in agreement.

"I recommend that you send out a forward party, General. Mounted riders can be there long before the sun sets. They can scout out the area and draw out a map of sorts. We can send a rider back with a dispatch detailing the layout."

"I see," the general muttered. "And I suppose you will want to be a part of the scouting party?"

Technically, the general couldn't prevent him from riding off. Trying to be diplomatic, Jonah replied, "With your permission, sir. I was thinking it might be like our days with General Wayne." This brought a smile to Harrison's face as Jonah hoped it would.

"Well, be off with you then; but what about the infantry? Have you forgotten about them?"

"No sir. I would rest them here about. Let them eat and rest and then move them out about midnight. That way, with a forced march, they would be close at dawn. They could rest a bit and still be ready to attack at first light. That is, if everything goes to plan."

"That damnable 'if'," Commodore Perry exclaimed. "There's always that."

"Yes, I like your plan to a point," Harrison said. "Colonel Johnson, pick your best men for scouts. We'll give the scouts a two hour head start. Then the mounted rifles will move out. As soon as you sight this McGregors Creek, you send a rider back to let the colonel know when he's close. That way, should you run into trouble, a suitable force will be close by to deal with it."

Jonah knew the change to his recommendation was so Harrison could say it was his plan of attack. It really didn't matter much, except now the mounted rifles as a group would have a cold camp that night. With the land open as this one was, a candle could be seen for miles.

As Jonah was mounting his horse, Gesslin rode up and said, "Thanks, friend." The words stung until Jonah saw Gesslin was smiling.

"You're most welcome," Jonah quipped. As he mounted, he said, "Ah... think of the glory. Captain Clay Gesslin, hero of McGregors Creek. He single-handedly took on the entire British garrison... and whipped them good."

"Gesslin for congress." This last was from Hampton, who hearing Jonah's tirade joined in. Gesslin's reply was not very complimentary.

"So you're riding with us?' Jonah asked and then realized it was a dumb question. Why else would Hampton be mounted if he wasn't to be part of the scouting party?

Taking a deep breath, Hampton exhaled and replied, "Someone who can draw a fair map and knows his letters has to attend you un-civilized souls."

"I see," Jonah said, then winking at Gesslin, he called to Moses. "You took any scalps lately, old friend?"

Having heard the good-natured bickering, Moses replied, "No, I ain't, but I'm itchin'."

"Well, it will be dark soon," Jonah said. "Lots of bad things happen in the dark."

Hampton swallowed hard and then turned in his saddle and spoke, "Moses, my old friend, would you care to ride along with me? Would you like some tobacco? I may have another bottle of wine tucked away if you'd care for a libation."

Looking back, Jonah said, "Moses can be had, James, but he ain't cheap. Keep talking though, likelihood is you'll keep your hair."

McGregors Creek turned out to be a tributary for the Thames River. The forward scouting party closed with it within three hours of leaving the main body of the mounted rifles. Gesslin sent a rider back a ways to wait on Colonel Johnson and then deployed his men to reconnoiter the area. The men moved off in twos with only their tomahawk and knives for weapons.

"I don't want some fool's gun going off," Gesslin had explained. "These men are seasoned backwoodsmen. They could kill you in your sleep and you wouldn't even know you were dead."

Still, it was a precaution and the men were professional enough not to argue. It was an hour after dark before all the scouting parties returned with a detailed report of what they had seen including men, arms, store-houses, and civilians.

"There's a bridge right here," one of the scouts was saying, pointing to a place on Hampton's map. "If we can take that, it'll be a lot easier getting across the creek. There is a village of sorts once you are past the creek."

"That's Chatham," Hampton said.

"Well, they's lots of folks about and even some this side of the creek."

When it was Jonah and Moses' turn to report, Jonah pointed to a spot on the map. "What's this area here?" he asked, knowing it was a junction of sorts.

"That's where a creek combines with the Thames River. Why do you ask?"

"There's a couple of keelboats or barges right there. I don't know what's loaded on them, but it must be important, as they are well-guarded. There was even a carriage pulled up next to one."

"Damn sir," Hampton cursed, all excited. "General Proctor travels in a carriage frequently. I'll bet it was him or his family."

"We didn't see no women or children," Moses volunteered and then added, "No Redcoat general either."

"Well, if there's a carriage, then he's close about," Hampton replied, refusing to relent. "If he's not, that's his belongings. I'd sure like to get aboard that boat. From the sound of these boys indicating the rest of the scouts, the rest of the places have a few soldiers here and there. But this place has a plenty. They are thicker than fleas on a hound's butt. I'd wait until tomorrow and have a bunch of soldiers there waiting for the attack. Maybe attack there first off."

"I dunno," the one scout replied. "Them boats might be important but taking that bridge would sure make it a lot easier .., specially for the infantry."

"I agree," Jonah said. "However, there's no reason the attack can't be from several directions at once."

I agree," Gesslin added. "I think we need to ride back and talk to the colonel first hand. There's too much to put into a dispatch."

"Clay," Hampton called to his friend. 'How about if I go and take...'"

"Moore's my name, sir, Arthur Moore.

"Yes, thank you. What if Moore and I ride back and talk with the colonel. Would that be satisfactory with you?"

"Yes, I think a verbal report would be much better," Gesslin replied. Then he added, "Even if the man writing the report is a man of letters."

"You devil," Hampton hissed. "Ready, Moore?"

The man nodded and the two men headed back to where the horses were being held.

"There's nothing to do now, men. We've done our job. Now it's sit back and wait," Gesslin said to his men.

"There's a place back yonder a ways, Captain, a deserted shack. It might be a better place to hole up. There are walls and a roof. That'll cut down on any wind and rain since we can't build no fire."

"Keep the frost off, too," Moses added.

"Is it where we can watch out for the Colonel?'

"Better than this heah place," Hicks said. "There is a stand of trees where we can tie a rope and hide the horses."

"All right, let's go."

The place was an old trapper's cabin. The floor was dirt with holes in the roof at places so you could see the sky. However, it was a lot better than being in the open or even under the trees. Some varmint had built a nest in the corner and there was a wood burning stove. Still, it was too dangerous to build a fire. If nothing else, the smoke might attract attention.

"Stove's pipes are probably stopped up by some critter anyway," Moses said.

Gesslin posted a guard on each side of the cabin so that anybody coming from either direction could be seen, and the horses could also be watched over as well. The men ate jerky and drank from their canteens.

Then, pulling their coats about them, they were soon asleep. *Tough, seasoned fighting men,* Jonah thought, as he pulled a blanket under his chin. These are the type of men this nation needs to survive. The politicians talked about freedom but these were the men who kept us free.

Little did Jonah know that back in Washington, Secretary of War Armstrong and President Madison were having a similar conversation at a dinner table set with fine china, crystal wine glasses, with beautiful ladies close by. They'd just finished a meal of lobster and steak and were waiting on dessert.

"Jonah's presence has kept things moving," President Madison said.

"Yes, Mr. President, its men like him who will help win this war and maintain our freedom."

Chapter Twenty-Eight

GENERAL HARRISON WAS WITH Johnson's mounted rifles when they arrived. A quick meeting took place with the leaders and a final plan of action was laid out. The attack would be pointed in three directions. One group would attack the storehouses, another group would secure the bridge, and the third group would attack the more heavily guarded barge.

The attack would take place at first light. Gesslin's scouts would sneak back in before daybreak and ascertain that things were as they had been last evening and that nothing had changed. If anything had changed, they would back out and warn the others if there was time. If not, a single shot would alert the group that something was amiss.

As the first rays of sun crept over the horizon, men mounted their horses. Little puffs of fog came from the animals as they snorted, and their hot breaths collided with the early morning chill. A heavy layer of frost covered the ground. Obvious tracks could be seen where the advanced party had walked through the frost, together at first and then separating into different directions. Jonah and Moses sat astride their horses ready to be off.

The man next to Jonah reached into a sack and pulled a twist of chewing tobacco out. He bit off a chew, and then, as he was putting the twist back into the sack, he addressed Jonah, "Care for a chew, Mr. Lee?"

"Thank you, no. I never chew before breakfast."

"Don't blame you," the man said, chewing on the twist. "Been known to turn a man's innards."

"I've heard the same thing," Jonah replied, not sure who he'd heard it from. In truth, he didn't chew but felt obliged to be diplomatic in his refusal.

"Sun is directly behind us," Moses volunteered.

That would mean the British would be looking directly into the sun as they approached. Visibility would be less, and the Americans would be on them before the British knew it. It had not been taken into consideration during the planning but was a definite advantage.

"Lord is looking after us," Moses commented.

`The word was given to move out, and the horses were walked until they reached the top of the rise overlooking the objective. Once there, they charged as a group and then at the last minute broke off into three separate groups. The British were ill-prepared for the attack. Complacency brought on by poor leadership, half rations, and a longing for home could all be cited as reason.

Not more than a dozen or so shots rang out as the mounted rifles swept down on the sleeping settlement. Most of the British soldiers put up very little fight. A few of the less demoralized set fire to a storage building. The soldiers guarding the keelboat and barge put up a stiff resistance, but the sheer number of Americans made it futile to continue. One brave soul did manage to set the barge on fire. With the storage house and barge on fire, the American army posted a guard on the British, and then the rest of the soldiers laid down their weapons and began fighting the fires.

With the Americans occupied, several Indians took the opportunity to attack the soldiers guarding the bridge and tried to destroy it. Soon, the rest of the Americans were alerted to the fight going on at the bridge and reinforced the soldiers there. Jonah and Moses were part of the relief column and soon found themselves under a withering fire. The Indians were putting up a much stiffer fight than the British had. Men were falling as ball after ball found its mark.

"They're in the trees," Jonah shouted to Moses.

A musket ball plowed into a bridge support Jonah was hiding behind. Sprayed by splinters from the wood, Jonah could feel the sting as they hit his face. Looking at the hole, it was obvious whoever fired the shot was in a higher position. That could only be the trees. No wonder the soldiers who thought they were under cover were falling.

Jonah watched the trees and was paid off for his vigilance. An Indian moved from where he'd been hiding to get a shot at some unsuspecting soldier. Jonah's long rifle was primed and loaded. Seeing the Indian move from behind the big branch, Jonah took quick aim and fired. His aim was true. The Indian jerked as the ball struck home, toppling the Indian backwards and out of the tree.

Grinning like a possum, Jonah yelled at his friend, "See that shot?"

"It was middling good," Moses shouted back then ducked as a ball kicked up dirt not a foot from him.

Jonah's eyes were starting to sting from the acrid gunpowder. There was little breeze about, and the fog of spent gunpowder was cutting down on visibility, making it difficult to see the enemy.

The battle had been going on over an hour when the Americans started fording the creek above and below the Indians to outflank them. As the soldiers started to close in, an Indian jumped from behind his cover and shouted defiantly at the Americans.

Realizing the brave was the leader of the Indian confederacy, Jonah took aim at the mighty Tecumseh, but before he could pull the trigger the Indian disappeared from sight. Frustrated, Jonah gave a yell and charged over the bridge. He was immediately followed by Moses and the Kentuckians. Coughing and choking from the smoke, they reached the other side of the bridge in time to see the Indian retreating on horseback.

With his chest heaving, one of the soldiers gasped, "This is why I'm not in the infantry."

Unable to speak, Jonah couldn't help but agree.

The fires on the barge and storehouse were put out, and General Harrison had parties of men led by an officer inspect and inventory the goods. The storehouse had been full of muskets, ammunition, and the last of the food that had been left for the garrison there. The inventory of the barge was much the same, except to the disappointment of Captain Hampton; the personal effects found on the barge were those of General Proctor's family.

Hampton did find out that General Proctor had left the previous morning. The area had been left under the command of Lieutenant Colonel Augustus Warburton. However, Lieutenant Colonel Warburton had gone up river to meet with General Proctor. It seemed the alliance with the Indians was falling apart. Tecumseh had sent Colonel Elliot to Lieutenant Colonel Warburton demanding to know where Proctor was going to take a stand and fight.

It seemed Moraviantown was the next likely place. With this information, General Harrison decided to rest his army the remainder of the day here. Tomorrow morning they would march to Moraviantown. *Will we meet the British there?* Jonah wondered. *Is that where Proctor will choose to make his stand?* One question after another filled his mind.

Walking to the creek, he passed three men covered with blankets. Good men who had given their all. The fight at the bridge would be listed as a skirmish if listed at all. However, three had paid the ultimate sacrifice. Six more were wounded. Would they be remembered in the same light as General Harrison or Commodore Perry? Not likely, yet they were just as important. Especially to the loved ones left behind.

They had salvaged over one thousand muskets in the storehouse that the British had tried to burn down.

But was all the muskets, the food, and bridge... worth even one life? Shaking his head, Jonah found it hard to justify. A gunshot rang out and Jonah was momentarily startled.

Moses spoke, explaining the gunshots. "The general must feel we'll meet the Redcoats tomorrow, as he has ordered several cows be slaughtered. The men will rest and eat well tonight."

"So the ice has melted," Jonah stated.

"I was thinking more like a last supper," Moses replied.

Chapter Twenty-Nine

CAMPFIRES LIT UP THE landscape as Harrison's army feasted on beef taken from farmer's pastures. Jonah, Moses, Clay Gesslin, and James Hampton had gathered around one of the fires on the outer perimeter, having had their fill of beef, fresh bread, and coffee. They lay on bedrolls with their belts loosened and moaning over having eaten too much.

"There's no way around it," Hampton was saying. "Proctor is running scared. He knows he has the whole American army after their Redcoat arses for letting the red devils slaughter our men at the River Raisin."

"I'm not so sure," Gesslin responded. "Those Indians of his put up a good fight at the bridge today."

"Huh!" Hampton snorted. "That was Tecumseh himself, not Proctor. You see what a job he did, took us two hours to overpower a handful of savages. It's a good thing he isn't calling the shots for the British; otherwise, we might be back in Detroit or Ohio somewhere."

"Well, Tecumseh has shown more leadership," Jonah said, speaking for the first time. "Think of all the stragglers and military stores we've taken with little or no opposition at all. We faced the most we've met today. Aside from the Indians, the British left such a weak guard there was little doubt they'd be taken."

"We should have already taken the British," Gesslin threw out.

"No," Jonah replied. "Not before taking control of the Great Lakes. Had we tried we may have faced a much different opposition."

"I agree with Jonah," Hampton said. "We had to take control of the overwater supply route."

"Well, tomorrow, we'll likely come face to face with General Proctor," Gesslin volunteered. "Colonel Johnson is convinced the British will have to stand and fight at Moraviantown. Not only are the Indians calling him a coward, but according to the troops we captured today, so are the officers. He'll have to make a stand soon or face a court martial and disgrace if not a firing squad."

"Shhh!" The men turned to Moses. "Riders coming," he said, "a large group."

The men quickly gathered their weapons, not sure if the riders were friendly or not. A challenge rang out in the dark. One of the sentries had stopped the riders. Soon, there was a call for the sergeant of the guards.

"Let's see what this is about," Gesslin said, and the group closed with the sentries. "What is it?" Gesslin asked as they approached, not wanting to startle a man with a loaded gun.

Actually, there were two men. One of them spoke, "Evening Captain. We got a whole passel of Injuns who want to see the general. The leader says they want to make a treaty."

"This sounds interesting," Hampton said. "Mr. Lee, maybe we should inform our leader and see if it's convenient for him to receive these noble warriors."

Harrison was more than eager to meet with the Indians. The Indian leader was Walk-in-the-Water, and with him rode sixty followers. It seems that they had also become very frustrated with the British and decided to make peace with the Americans. A big to-do was made over their decision to desert the British. Food was served in great quantity but no alcohol was given, much to the Indians' disappointment. The Americans, Harrison promised, would always be friends with the Indians and not turn their back as the Redcoats had done.

During the pow-wow, Walk-in-the-Water confirmed General Proctor had given his word to Tecumseh that they would fight. Just outside of Moraviantown was where they would make their stand.

A thick swamp was to one side and the Thames River on the other. That left a narrow passage that would be easy to defend. Harrison immediately made plans to move out at daybreak. He was also assigning Colonel Wood the job to reconnoiter the areas Walk-in-the-Water had described. Little did Harrison and the American army know, but they were being scouted also.

Tecumseh and General Proctor descended the river very quietly and made a reconnaissance of Harrison's camp. After seeing the outlay of the camp, Tecumseh wanted to spring a surprise attack. Proctor refused, feeling it would be dishonorable, stating they would meet the enemy at Moraviantown.

Angry with Proctor for his unwillingness to attack, Tecumseh decided to stay close and keep a watch over the American army. He and a few of his chiefs spent the night at the house of a friendly mill owner. If Harrison's army headed toward Moraviantown, he would gallop ahead and warn the British.

Rumors quickly spread throughout the encampment: the Shawnee's are surrendering. Before that rumor could be dispelled, and the truth that only sixty or so had decided not to fight was made known, than the whispered rumors spread that they'd meet the British come tomorrow.

Jonah and Moses made their way back to the campsite. "Do you think it will be tomorrow?" Jonah asked his friend.

"If not tomorrow, then the next day," Moses replied. Both men knew Proctor could not continue to run.

"We've covered a lot of ground in the last few days in our attempt to bring the British to battle. Now that it's almost here, I thought I'd be excited," Jonah admitted to his friend. "However, all I am is tired."

"It's not just the travel," Moses said. "It's also the weather. I don't 'spect you're any different than most. We are all bone weary." Stretching out on his bedroll and pulling his blanket up to his chin, Moses gave a sigh. "That little trapper's cabin was a sight better than this," meaning sleeping under the stars. "We could have even built a fire tonight."

"True," Jonah replied, with a yawn and then continued, "However, it's on the other side of the creek. You want to ride back over there? Moses!"

The only reply Jonah got was the constant sound of a deep sleep. *Apparently, I'm not the only one tired*, he thought as he closed his eyes.

The gray light of dawn was making its way on the eastern horizon. Men moved as shadows. Breakfast had already been eaten, horses saddled, and fires put out.

"Notice the general's personal belongings are all being put into one of the wagons that will be in the rear."

Moses nodded but didn't reply.

Gesslin, with a company of mounted rifles, had been assigned the point once again. "Problem is," Gesslin snorted, "once they learn your name, they can't forget it. Means we got to go to bed earlier so we can get up earlier, and if you don't move quick-like, it means you get no coffee."

So that's it, Jonah thought. *Gesslin hasn't had his coffee*. As the riders made their way out of the field in which they had camped, lights could be seen from a farmhouse. The lowing of cows could be heard.

"Ready for milking," Moses volunteered.

No sooner had he spoken, than a man with a lantern walked out of a back door and headed toward a barn. As the mounted rifles drew abreast of the house, a woman rushed from the house. She looked both ways nervously as Gesslin halted the riders. She was obviously frightened, and the way she kept looking side to side, she was afraid she was being watched. By who was the question... was it the enemy, her husband or who?

"Sir," she whispered. "There's a bunch of those red devils lying in wait. They plan to ambush you when you pass by. I... just wanted you to know, sir." Then the lady dashed back into the house.

Gesslin motioned the company to move out but didn't speak until they were several hundred yards down the road, and then he halted the column again. "Men, did you hear?" he asked. "There's an ambush up ahead. I don't know how she knows, but as skittish as she was, I believe her. We've been warned now. We will split into two columns, one on the right under Mr. Lee, and I'll take the left side. First sign of trouble we ride like hell. Shoot anything that moves... except me or Mr. Lee." This brought a chuckle as Gesslin knew it would. "Any questions?"

When none were asked, he wheeled his horse around and men rode left and right. The sun was rising now and a small creek could be seen just ahead.

"Likely spot," Jonah volunteered.

"My thoughts as well," Gesslin replied.

Several clicks could be heard as men eased the hammers back on their long rifles. Obviously, they felt the same way. Still, the men eased along as if they had not a care in the world. The cry of a war whoop was heard as a Shawnee brave dashed out of the woods wielding a war ax. Moses' gun was lying across his saddle with the barrel pointing toward the brave. He simply pulled the trigger and the warrior was knocked backwards, a huge hole in his chest. Several shouts and war whoops were heard as the Indians rose up from their hiding places to fire at the Americans.

When the mounted rifles dug into the flanks of their horses and charged, the Indians panicked and tried to retreat. However, the Kentuckians rode them down. A few of the riders were pulled from their horses by the braves, but another rider was right there to help.

Instead of the Americans, it was the Indians who were taken completely by surprise. In no time, the Indians had been easily dispatched, with only a few minor wounds to the mounted rifles. What should not have shocked Jonah but did was the number of Indian scalps hanging from rifle barrels. Tired they may be, these men were ready to fight. Anybody who didn't believe it had only to look at the dripping scalps.

Chapter Thirty

AFTER THE SKIRMISH WITH the Indians, the point riders rode without mishap for the next ten miles. Seeing riders ahead, the point man signaled the rest of the group, who quickly found cover. There were three riders in the group.

Seeing it was Hampton, Jonah called out from his position but didn't show himself immediately. "You there... hold up." The surprise was complete. Then, before showing himself, Jonah spoke out, "A man of words you may be, but not a man of the woods."

Riding out from his cover, he spoke again. "It's a hellish brave man, you are. If we'd been Tecumseh's Indians, you'd be scalped by now."

As other men rode out shaking their fresh scalps to emphasize Jonah's point, Hampton swallowed hard.

"We were told to expect you," Colonel Woods said, taking advantage of his rank.

"So were those," Jonah replied, nodding toward the dangling scalps. He was not concerned about the colonel or his rank, but hated to think how easily they could have lost their lives had his group been Indians.

"Had you run up on the same bunch as we did," Gesslin said, backing up Jonah. "You would likely be goners or making your report to General Proctor instead of General Harrison." The colonel and Hampton were quick to realize their blunder.

"How far back is General Harrison?" Colonel Woods asked.

"I'm not sure, sir," Gesslin replied, now all military. "They were to be about an hour back but that was before we were set upon. After jawing with you these past few minutes, I'd say they can't be more than half an hour behind."

"I see," the colonel said. "There's a small creek not a mile back the way we came. We will go back to it and wait for the general," Colonel Woods said, giving orders to Gesslin. "From that point to the British line is less than... three miles... wouldn't you say, Captain Hampton?"

"There about," Hampton replied. Colonel Woods, Hampton, and a sergeant had ridden out last evening to meet up with other spies who were keeping a close eye on the British army. They were now on their way back to report their findings to General Harrison.

Reaching the creek, the horses were watered, and men rested on the creek bank, holding the reins to their mounts. Not trusting to chance, Gesslin deployed several guards. Soon, gunfire could be heard, but it didn't have the back and forth that was usual in a battle. Nor were there any other sounds that would be associated with a fight.

Seeing Jonah's look, Gesslin answered the unasked question. "Colonel Johnson is firing shots around the horse's heads. He's getting them used to the noise so they won't spook during battle. The colonel heard of a general who was on a fox hunt once. He had this beautiful jumper, but when they blew the horns for the hunt to begin, that blame horse reared up and dumped his master right in a pile of fresh horse dung. Said neither the general nor the horse was fit to hunt. Colonel Johnson is ready to hunt Redcoats, and he wants his horses just as ready."

Trying not to laugh, Colonel Woods said, "You don't expect me to believe that tale do you, Captain Gesslin?"

"Well sir," Gesslin said, pausing as if pondering his next words. Finally, he said, "It's between you and Colonel Johnson whether you believe the story or not. However, I suspect if you were to ask his father-in-law, you better have a fast horse ready."

"No, Captain, I'll take your word for it."

Once the colonel had ambled off, Jonah sidled up to Gesslin and said, "I didn't know Colonel Richard Mentor Johnson had a wife or family."

Gesslin looked straight at Jonah and replied, "He doesn't."

"You sod," Jonah said, laughing. "Does Hampton know?"

"Course he does. You want to make a bet on if Woods will ask Johnson?"

"No, I don't believe I'll take that bet."

Seeing Hicks walk up, Gesslin acknowledged the man. "Rest of the outfit is coming, sir."

"Thank you, Hicks. Now let's see what our masters have up their sleeves, Mr. Lee." As Gesslin walked by, Jonah thumped him a good one as he fell in step behind his friend.

Colonel Woods was laying out Proctor's line of defense. "He has a six-pounder about here," he was saying, "but they've put up no breast-work. Also, Proctor's men are drawn up in open lines, separated from one another instead of standing close together or in ranks. Of course, we need to test their lines to see if they'll remain the same once the fighting starts."

The colonel's map was drawn up much as they were told with the river on the right, the swamp on the left, and the British in the middle.

"But where are Tecumseh's warriors?" Someone asked the question that was on Jonah's mind.

Unlike the 'we aren't sure' reply that was given, Jonah was sure. The Indians would be in the swamp. He wasn't sure what it would take to overrun the British. Probably not much if what they'd encountered the last few days was a true example. But the Indians, that would be another story. Before this day was done, there would be more American blood mixed with the Canadian soil. Would some of it be his or Moses? Only God knew.

There would be no more postponement, no more maneuvering. Today was the day. Before the sun went down, they'd either be victorious... or possibly dead. Forlorn hope... *What is that?* Jonah wondered. His mind had drifted away and now they were talking of a forlorn hope.

"A group of twenty riders or so," the general was saying, "can charge the British, and then when the British respond, the riders can cut off the charge."

"Cut off the charge?" Jonah said aloud. "General, you might stop a horse but you can't stop a cannon ball or musket ball once it's fired."

"I am aware of that," Harrison snorted.

"Then you are just as aware that you are sending twenty men to a certain death."

"We have to know how Proctor's forces will be deployed, Mr. Lee."

"General, with all due respect, from what we've seen these last few days, you can't expect much."

"Dregs sir," someone unseen had spoken.

"They now have leadership," General Harrison replied. "We have to know if they intend to do battle as they appear or not."

Angered beyond control, Jonah spoke, "Then I request permission to lead the charge, sir."

"Request denied."

"But sir!"

"Don't push me, Jonah," Harrison snapped. "By God, we've been friends for a long time and because of that I've made allowances. But you will not challenge me on this. We already have our volunteers. They are ready and that puts an end to it."

Jonah started to speak again but felt a hand on his arm. Turning, he saw Colonel Richard Johnson and next to him, Moses. Johnson gave Jonah a firm look, motioned to the general with his eyes and then squeezed Jonah's arm, giving another firm look.

"My apologies, General," Jonah finally said.

"Think nothing of it," Harrison replied. "Your hearts in the right place, regardless of the politics."

Walking away from the general's group, Johnson whispered, "You are right, but we are too close to putting an end to it to have the general get mad and put you under house arrest."

"He couldn't...," Jonah started, but Johnson cut him off.

"He could. It's a long way to Washington. You've done a good job but don't push it. You can't change it and making a scene will only make matters worse. Besides that, you wouldn't be able to live with yourself if you were kept out of the battle because you were being bull-headed. You've apologized, now let it go."

"Hell man, I'd beg and crawl if I had to."

"I am sure you would, Jonah," Johnson said. "Besides, it's a sound military strategy. No one will fault the general for his forlorn hope."

"I'm not thinking of fault, I was thinking of lives."

"What about the lives saved if the general is right, and they've other men deployed that we can't see? It's a necessary evil."

"You're right," Jonah acknowledged and then went to find Moses.

Seeing a group of men passing a jug, Jonah knew these had to be the volunteers. Among them was William Whitley. It was said he built the first brick house in Kentucky. He had enlisted as a private at age sixty-four. William was a man who was welcomed at any campfire. *He should be at home in his rocking chair*, Jonah thought.

"Jonah!" Turning, he saw that it was Moses speaking to him. "Colonel Richard Johnson has invited us to ride with the mounted rifles today. He says we are honorary Kentuckians now, and it wouldn't be right to go into battle with any other group."

"I'll be glad to ride with the colonel, but nothing says you have to. In fact, nothing says you have to go into battle at all."

"You are going," Moses replied. "So I'm going."

"You have always been at my side," Jonah said, trying to control his emotions. "There has never been a time when you weren't there for me."

"And you for me," Moses said, cutting off his friend's remarks. Then before Jonah could speak, Moses continued, "The colonel has ordered his men to arm themselves with rifles, knives, and tomahawks. No swords or pistols."

"I see," Jonah replied. "Well, let's be fetching our weapons."

"We'll need to check the edges as well," Moses added.

Chapter Thirty-One

IT WAS MIDDAY WHEN twenty Americans mounted their horses to charge the British lines. Hands were shaken and men joked about, each knowing this may be the last ride many of them would take.

"Well, let's be about it," a sergeant said, addressing the riders.

A group of mounted rifles rode with the men of the forlorn hope to a point some three to four hundred yards from the British lines.

Seeing the forlorn hope riders line up, Tecumseh used the distraction to cross the Thames River by a ford and made his way to the swamp where his warriors waited. In passing, he saw General Proctor and called out, "Father! Have a big heart."

Once at the edge of the swamp, an air of melancholy fell over the chief. He had fought many a battle and had never received much more than a scratch. However, today he would die. It did not make him sad; he was a warrior. Perhaps, it was hearing one of Proctor's officers say it was downright murder to fight from such a vulnerable spot as Proctor had chosen.

Looking about, Tecumseh saw the British officer. Taking a page from the Indians, he had deployed two hundred men from the forty-first regiment inside the tree line where there was plenty of cover.

Back at the American lines, horses pawed, pranced, and whinnied. One or two tried to bite their neighbor, but the firm hands holding the reins would pull until the bit would bite into the horse's mouth and the animal would forget about its neighbor.

General Harrison had ridden to the front line and spoke with each of the men. When that was done, he gave a nod and the sound of charge rang out from the bugle. The pounding of horses hooves made the ground vibrate. The British had been expecting the attack, but the sound of the bugle and the thunder of charging horses scared more than one man. Several of them would have run had not their sergeants and officers been there, cursing and driving them back to their post.

Hair raising yells filled the air as the riders galloped toward the British lines. General Proctor was behind the British line shouting encouragement.

A British officer called out, "Down in front, all right lads, take aim, steady, steady, I say... fire."

The entire front line fired, sending a swarm of musket balls to meet the rushing riders. The sounds of balls plowing into flesh made a sickening thud. The riders did their job, but too well. Cries of pain filled the air as both men and horses were hit with the onslaught of lead, buzzing like a swarm of angry hornets. Riders fell from their horses and lay dead. A wounded horse tried to rise several times, and finally a shot rang out from the edge of the woods putting the animal out of its misery.

From the American lines not a man spoke. General Harrison saw Jonah but would not make eye contact. A few of the men who survived the charge could be seen standing or trying to stand. One man was helping a friend on a horse.

A British soldier raised his musket to fire, only to be called down by his sergeant. "As you were, Lewis."

Of the twenty riders who rode with the forlorn hope, fifteen were killed outright and four were wounded. Only one man survived without even a scratch. With tears running down his face, he helped his wounded comrades back to their lines. One of the fallen was the sixty-four year old, William Whitley. An eerie silence hung over the Americans for a time.

Having discovered how Proctor had arrayed his troops, General Harrison held an officer's call. "Colonel Johnson, form your regiment on the left flank and I will bring up the infantry and attack the British line."

Johnson was ecstatic and thanked General Harrison for giving his men the tougher assignment. Johnson immediately sent a lieutenant to find a way into the swamp. Meanwhile, Commodore Perry realizing the cavalry, as he called the mounted rifles, would be leading the attack, positioned himself next to Lieutenant Colonel James Johnson. Governor Shelby's militia would support the mounted rifles as he saw fit.

As the final preparations were being made, Johnson's lieutenant returned and reported, "I have scouted the swamp and find it impassable."

When General Harrison was made aware of the situation, a look of dismay filled his face. "Very well, Colonel, pull your men back and act as a reserve." Harrison's demeanor stung Johnson's pride. The general as much as said he was a coward.

Unable to stand such a blight, intentional or not, Johnson replied with a firmness he had not used on the general previously. "General Harrison, permit me to charge the enemy, and the battle will be won in thirty minutes."

Harrison was again dismayed at the way Johnson had spoken to him. Angrily, he replied, *"Damn them! Charge them!"* The general then turned abruptly to inform Governor Shelby and the other officers that he had changed the battle plan.

Colonel Richard Johnson made his way to tell his brother of the change when he was called by his aide. Turning, Johnson found not only his aide, but Jonah and Moses.

"We've found a place to cross into the swamp, after all."

"Damnation," Johnson roared. "Jonah, you've made my day."

Lieutenant Colonel James Johnson had heard the interchange. Seeing his brother and his nephews standing behind their father, Colonel Richard Johnson made a quick unauthorized decision.

However, if the plan was put into effect quickly, General Harrison would not have time to countermand his order.

"Brother," Johnson said. "Take my place at the head of the first battalion and charge the British. I will cross the swamp and fight the Indians with the second."

Jonah, Moses, and the officers of both battalions stood, their mouths agape. They couldn't help but feel proud. They all knew Richard Johnson was assigning himself the greater risk.

James Johnson and his sons started to protest, but Richard, placing his hand on his brother's shoulder, cut off the words. "Brother," Richard said, motioning to James' sons with his eyes said, "You have a family, and I have none."

Not trusting his emotions to speak, James swallowed and then turned, "First battalion, prepare to charge."

Chapter Thirty-Two

I T WAS 2:30 P.M. when the American army formed up to attack. Lieutenant James Johnson had his mounted rifles on the left, along with Governor Shelby's division. General Harrison lined up his infantry on the right side. In the distance, behind the British line, General Proctor could be seen riding among his men, urging them to stand fast.

The powder smoke from the muskets fired at the 'forlorn hope' had been swept away by a gentle breeze. With a nod from General Harrison, the bugler's nervous lips blew the bugle. As the charge was sounded, riders kneed their mounts and horses bounded away.

The British infantry watched the thundering riders approach. Unlike the 'forlorn hope' riders' small line, this group was so big, there was little doubt that the British line would be overrun. To add to the frightening sight of a charging brigade, a yell came from the group that was taken up and repeated time and time again. "Remember the Raisin! Remember the Raisin!" Closer the charging riders came.

"Wait... wait," a British officer spoke to his men in a trembling voice that could not hide his anxiety. He, like several of his Grenadiers, had been at the "Battle of the River Raisin." They had marched away before the Indians butchered the wounded prisoners, but he'd heard of the ungodly acts and knew in his heart the lack of vigilance in keeping the wounded prisoners safe would come back to haunt them.

The honor of the battle had been lost by the atrocities of the savages. Now, they would have to answer for their injustice. Would anyone survive? Would those that survived write his parents and say Lieutenant Richard Bullock died bravely fighting for king and country?

The sound of the bugle continued to blast. The riders were now two hundred yards away, one hundred fifty, seventy-five, and fifty. Clods of dirt were flying in the air from the horses hooves as froth flew from the mouths of the wild-eyed steeds. The screaming riders rode with reckless abandon. Today the British would pay. A Brown Bess smooth bore musket fired from the British line; a nervous soldier with an itchy trigger finger.

"Take that man's name, Sergeant," an officer ordered.

A chuckle was heard down the line. "Damn, little good that will do," another soldier said.

"Ready," the British officer roared out, yelling to be heard above the thundering drum of horse's hooves. "Aim... fire!!!"

The first volley emptied a few saddles but did nothing to slow the charging Americans. British Lieutenant Bullock found himself yelling, "Fire the cannon! Fire the bloody cannon."

As close packed as the riders were, it would surely disrupt the charge. *Where is Proctor?* Bullock wondered. He should be directing the British defense. The roar of muskets being fired was deafening as the British got off its second volley, but it did nothing to slow the onslaught of determined American riders.

The British infantry was busy trying to reload their Brown Bess muskets when the charging riders pierced the line and then wheeled, pouring a destructive fire into the British. The infantry lost its composure and men began to break ranks and flee. A few were tied up in hand to hand combat, but by now, the second wave of the riders had surrounded the British.

Seeing the British were beaten and further fighting would only result in useless death, Governor Isaac Shelby shouted, "Surrender! Surrender! There's no use resisting, you are surrounded."

A British officer, seeing the battle was lost, threw down his sword and raised his hands. Seeing the officer surrender, the other soldiers laid down their weapons, knowing the battle was over.

The American infantry had now rushed up on the line and began collecting weapons.

"Where is Proctor?" General Harrison asked. His answer came from a British officer.

"We'd like to know the same damn thing, General."

Finally, a British colonel said, "The coward, with a company of dragoons and savages, were seen escaping toward Moraviantown."

"Ten minutes, sir," Lieutenant Colonel James Johnson spoke to General Harrison.

"What's that?" Harrison asked.

"Ten minutes, sir. Richard said we'd defeat the British line in thirty minutes. We did it in one-third the time."

"Well that's fine, Colonel," Harrison replied. "But is that not the sound of gunfire coming from the swamp?"

Governor Shelby was within hearing distance of the exchange. "I've sent my men to the swamp to aid Colonel Johnson," he stated. "They are likely having a much harder go of it fighting the Shawnee hidden in the swamp."

While the three men had been talking, the sound of gunfire had picked up, and so had the sound of yells, curses, and war whoops. *Men are fighting and dying in the swamp*, James Johnson thought. *And all I could think of was that we defeated the British line in ten minutes. The war, however, was not yet won. God be with Richard and his men*, he prayed.

Chapter Thirty-Three

WHEN THE BUGLE BLASTED the charge for the assault on the British lines, Colonel Richard Mentor Johnson's brigade made their way into the swamp. Smiling at Jonah, Johnson said, "I predict a hot day, Mr. Lee." The colonel was not talking about the weather.

"I expect you are right," Jonah replied.

Riding double behind him, Moses grunted, "Not too hot, I hope."

Because of the thick undergrowth which gave limited access, the brigade doubled the amount of men it could bring into action by each horse carrying two men. Also, due to the tangled thickets, swords were left at camp. Each man carried, beside his rifle, a hatchet and a knife. Moses had sharpened Jonah's and his edged weapons the night before. In fact, men had watched and emulated the man from Washington and his friend. Each carried two knives and two tomahawks. It was the second tomahawk that was poking into Moses' back, creating a bad humor.

The sound of bugles blaring, charging horses, and musket fire was heard on the road, but everything was quiet in the swamp; too quiet.

"I feel like we're being watched," Moses whispered.

"So do I," Jonah replied, waiting for shots to ring out.

Deeper they rode, the horses hooves now sinking into the soft wet ground. Men were fighting the vines and tangled thickets to keep from being knocked off their mounts. Tecumseh chose his line of defense well. He waited patiently, and when Johnson's men were preoccupied with the undergrowth, he let out a blood-curdling war cry and guns blazed away as warriors fired from their hiding places.

It was not unlike stumbling into a hornet's nest as balls buzzed through the air. Some hit trees, showering bark into the faces of men and horses. Others found their mark, as the unmistakable sound of lead balls thudded into human flesh. At the front of the line, Richard Johnson was hit twice, in the hip and the thigh. Though unable to dismount himself, he shouted out the order.

"Dismount... dismount!"

The men didn't need to be told. Most had already slid off their mounts seeking cover. One horse stung by flying bark became wild-eyed. With nostrils flaring, it reared up and toppled its rider into a pool of muck. A ball then struck the frightened animal, grazing its hind quarters and causing it to run wildly into the swamp, knocking over a warrior who tried to catch the animal as a prize.

Seeing Johnson was wounded, Jonah and Moses darted from tree to tree to get to the brigade's leader. The fire from the Indians continued with deadly accuracy and effect. Few of the Indians were showing themselves, and to make matters worse, Redcoats were now running into the swamp. Was it a planned attack or were the Redcoats retreating from the battle on the road? Regardless of the reason, the red uniforms made better targets than the brown-skinned warriors and the Americans took advantage of the targets.

Like their comrades on the road, the Kentuckians began to cry out, "Remember the Raisin, Remember the Raisin." This cry seemed to rally the Kentuckians, who were now finding targets other than the red uniforms. Firing their long rifles, men used them as clubs or laid them aside in favor of the tomahawk and knife. Remembering their fellow Kaintucks, who these savages had so ruthlessly slaughtered, the men fought with reckless abandon. Steel clanged on steel as knives flashed and tomahawks thudded into flesh and bone.

Unlike their British counterparts, the Shawnee braves were putting up a fierce battle. Jonah was on top of a warrior when another jumped him from behind. Unfortunately, for the brave, Moses was close, having just dispatched his foe. Making a half-turn, he grabbed the Indian's wrist as he raised his knife to stab Jonah. Feeling the grip on his wrist, the Indian spun. As he did so, Moses struck with all his might driving the tomahawk deep into the enemy's face and skull. Eyes glazing over, the Indian fell dead.

Tecumseh's shouts egging his warriors on could be heard above the melee. Taking a second to peer about him, Jonah was shocked to see Colonel Johnson still mounted and wounded in several places. "Follow me," he yelled to Moses as he made his way to the colonel.

He'd never survive if he stayed mounted. He was too much of a target. Then, before his very eyes, Jonah saw a puff of blood and dust jump from Johnson's body as another ball had found its mark. Jonah's stomach felt sickened. He could not let such a brave man die. Rushing to the aid of the colonel, Jonah and Moses found themselves attacked by a swarm of braves.

Shots rang out and three Indians fell; each had been hit several times. Blood splattered across Moses' buckskin shirt. Wiping it away, he was glad it wasn't his. The two remaining braves, seeing their companions down, fled into the swamp. Another shot was heard and a ball ricocheted into the ground beside Moses. Damned if the colonel hadn't been right. It had gotten hot...hot as Hades.

Taking time to reload his long rifle, Jonah saw that more Americans were making their way into the swamp. It was their fire that downed the three Indians. Now the battle was turning for the Americans. Jonah couldn't help but admire the gallant defense put up by the Indians. Hopping over logs and ducking underbrush, he and Moses made their way to the colonel.

Above the din of battle, a lone war cry went up above all else. Tecumseh, wounded but still fighting, had spotted Colonel Johnson and was taking aim at him. Wounded as he was, Johnson had little strength left, but he was trying to raise his own rifle. Jonah and Moses, seeing the proud Indian chief raise his weapon to fire, quickly aimed and fired their long rifles. Another shot was heard as Colonel Johnson's weapon went off. Unable to bring the long rifle to bear, the shot went off into the ground, harmlessly.

Seeing the great chief's body jerk as two balls plowed into the warrior's chest, Johnson looked toward Jonah and Moses. As smoke drifted from the barrels of the men's guns, a look of gratitude passed between the men.

The fever of battle was still burning, and one of the Kentuckians yelled out, "The colonel has just killed Tecumseh." He'd heard the shot, he'd seen the colonel's weapon lower and he'd seen the Indian chief fall. He'd not seen Jonah and Moses as the colonel's horse blocked them from his view.

Hearing the man shout out caused two things to happen: the Indians either threw down their weapon and surrendered or ran off into the swamp. The second thing caused by the shout was men rushed to the spot where Tecumseh fell, and remembering their fallen comrades, began to hack and cut away pieces of the chief, mutilating his body beyond recognition. To try to stop the savagery was a useless effort. Jonah and Moses looked on with disgust.

The chief had fought a brave fight and didn't deserve such an ending. *Had the British forces been led by General Brock along with Tecumseh and the Shawnee warriors, things might have turned out much differently,* Jonah thought. Men were now gathering around Colonel Johnson. Clay Gesslin was there, as was his man, Hicks. Both were dirty with powder-stained faces. Blood and grime covered their hands, but neither seemed wounded.

Jonah and Moses helped Gesslin and Hicks pull the pain stricken Johnson from his horse. The white horse was now streaked with blood from the colonel's wounds. Grim faced, Johnson looked to Jonah, "You are unhurt, Mr. Lee... Moses?"

"We are fine," Jonah replied for both of them.

As Major Barry, Johnson's secretary, wrapped a blanket about the colonel, Johnson gritted his teeth and managed, "I fear I have been cut to pieces, but I think my vitals have escaped."

Indeed, the colonel had been 'cut to pieces,' as he said. He had five wounds. As the surgeon arrived, Johnson looked at Jonah and said, "Sir, I will forever be in your debt." The pain was so obvious; it took a great effort for Johnson to speak.

Knowing what the colonel meant but was not spoken, Jonah only nodded. As they moved the colonel, Johnson spoke to his secretary again, "Have a heart, Barry, I will not die."

The surgeon, A.J. Mitchell, felt his body shiver realizing he would be blamed if the colonel didn't pull through. In the distance, an episodic shot could be heard as Major David Thompson chased the retreating Indians.

"Chase they might," Moses said, "but they'd not likely catch the retreating Shawnee."

From the edge of the swamp, men cheered as Johnson was brought out. "Three cheers for Colonel Johnson, the man who killed Tecumseh."

"Reckon he'll ever give you the credit?" Surprised, Jonah and Moses turned. "I saw it," Captain Clay Gesslin said. "He shouldn't take the credit."

"So far, I haven't heard him do so," Jonah remarked.

"He ain't said he didn't," Gesslin replied, staunch in his belief.

"He won't." Again the three men turned. It was Captain Hampton. In searching for his friends, he'd heard the exchange. "He needs the political recognition that will come from being known as the man that killed Tecumseh. He might even ride the reputation to the White House. You don't have any political aspirations, do you, Jonah?"

Shaking his head, Jonah replied, "None."

"Then you shouldn't mind, sir, as your silence will give you a powerful man as an ally. Believe me, gentlemen, if he lives, Johnson will one day be a powerful man."

Epilogue

ONCE BACK ON THE main road, Jonah's group was spotted by Lieutenant Colonel James Johnson. As the colonel rode over to the men, he inquired about his brother. After hearing of his wounds, Johnson rode off to where the surgical tent had been set up. The surgeons from both armies were busy caring for the wounded, regardless of their uniform.

As Johnson rode off, Jonah looked up at the still mounted Commodore Perry. He had been at Lieutenant Colonel James Johnson's side since the first bugle had sounded.

"Well Commodore, "Jonah said with a smile. "Are you ready to give up your ships and sails for the Calvary?"

Chuckling, the commodore shook his head. "It's been exciting. and I wouldn't have missed it for the world." Then, with his feet in the stirrups, he rose up and pulled at his trousers adding, "But I don't think my bottom could stand much more." This brought about the laugh as he knew it would.

As soldiers drifted out of the swamp, one of Gesslin's men approached and volunteered, "Did you hear, sir? Not only did we get Tecumseh, but we killed six other chiefs as well. One of them is said to be Tecumseh's brother-in-law, Wahsikegaboe (Firm Fellow). He was married to Tecumapeace, who was Tecumseh's sister."

I wonder how he knows that, Jonah thought. But the man answered the question before it was asked.

"Most of the Indians ran off carrying as many of their wounded as possible. But one of the captured Indians is being taken around, and he's identifying those left behind, both the dead and wounded.

The sun was starting to go down when the patrol Harrison sent after General Proctor returned. They had not been able to overtake the British general, but they were able to capture his baggage train, which Proctor had not spared the time or men for. Going through the confiscated possessions, Harrison's men collected personal papers and dispatches, which Harrison decided to forward on to Washington.

In a jovial mood after winning the battle, Harrison sent for Jonah. "Well, old friend," he greeted Jonah. "I see we've made it through another campaign. I feel we have broken the British hold on the northwest, and I'm about to send dispatches to that effect to Washington. I'm still waiting on an accurate count of men killed, wounded, and prisoners captured to include in that dispatch. That will give you time to write your own report so the rider can include it in his bag."

This was a kind offer, Jonah realized. Harrison was offering the proverbial 'olive branch.' Why shouldn't he? The campaign had been won. Not much of a battle in one sense, but a great victory in another.

"Thank you, sir. I will write a brief report. General," Jonah spoke again.

"Yes," Harrison replied.

"My congratulations, sir; I salute you."

Moved by Jonah's remarks, Harrison responded, "You were a big part of it, old friend. Let not a few words spoken in anger at heated times come between us."

"Thank you," Jonah replied.

Later, by the heat of a flickering campfire, drinking strong black coffee, Hampton was quoting figures to his friends. "We've been able to count thirty-three dead Indians, and there's no telling how many of them the retreating Indians dragged away. However, when we went back for Tecumseh's body it was nowhere to be found."

"I'm sure some of his braves snuck back and took the body," Moses volunteered.

"Regardless, we'll pack up and head home tomorrow."

"Tomorrow!" Jonah repeated.

"Yes," Hampton replied. "Harrison has nailed shut the door the Commodore closed. Harrison will reinforce strategic forts and will push on with a large force making sure the British don't mount a counter offensive. But for most of the volunteer militia, the war is over. Governor Shelby is taking his boys home tomorrow; their moment of glory is over."

"I think we shall ride with them, at least as far as Sandwich," Jonah replied. "Plan on spending some time there, do you?" Gesslin jokingly said to his friend.

"One never knows," Jonah returned, but his mind was firmly set on a lovely widow who said she'd be waiting.

Without another word, Moses went about packing their belongings and thinking they'd more likely-than-not meet up with some of the Indian women who responded so positive to his protection. Downright grateful they were!

Historical Notes

This book was written to honor the 200th anniversary of America's second revolution. The forgotten conflict as it is called by some. Tom Grundner and I talked about the upcoming 200th anniversary, and it was his encouragement that was the deciding factor for me to agree to write a trilogy on the war.

With the exception of my characters, I tried to remain true, good or bad, to the leaders of the war. The battles from Frenchtown and the massacre at the River Raisin, to the attack at Fort Stephenson; and the last big battle outside of Moraviantown were as historically accurate as possible. The ship to ship battles on the Great Lakes where Commodore Perry defeated the British naval commander, Captain Barclay followed the history books very closely.

The description of the landscape and the elements endured by our fighting men was as close to the actual events as I could make it. Of course, this is a work of fiction, so I did take certain liberties. There was no way to put a real life person at all the historically significant events, hence the creation of the president's man. A person who had a certain degree of freedom to move about as he wished and could travel to hot spots as the need arose.

The following books in the trilogy will deal with the Battle of Horseshoe Bend and include the fall of Washington. The last book will be based on the Battle of New Orleans.

For anyone interested in reading more on the War of 1812, I highly recommend the following books:

Kentucky in the War of 1812 by Anderson, Chenault, Quisenberry

The War of 1812, a Forgotten Conflict by Donald R. Hickey

1812, the War that Forged a Nation by Walter R. Borneman

Union 1812 by A.J. Langguth

Warships of the Great Lakes 1754-1834 by Robert Malcomson

About the Author

Michael Aye is a retired Naval Medical Officer. He has long been a student of early American and British Naval history. Since reading his first Kent novel, Mike has spent many hours reading the great authors of sea fiction, often while being "haze gray and underway" himself. This is his first novel on the War of 1812.

Acknowledgements

American authors, Jim Nelson and Bill Hammond, continue to lend an ear and offer advice and wisdom to a novice. I feel that they set the standard by which the rest of us strive to reach. Thanks for always being there.

British author, Alaric Bond, has become a good friend. His in-depth knowledge and willingness to share information about the business has been heartfelt. Alaric's unique style and deviation from the usual format for his characters place him in a category by himself and in line with the masters of nautical fiction.

To Chris Lindensmith of Bitingduck. This is our first work together and it has been a pleasure.

The availability of this work is totally due to the dedication and tireless efforts of my writing partner and my partner in life. Her name should come first.

Lightning Source UK Ltd.
Milton Keynes UK
UKOW05f2044101113

220777UK00008B/122/P

9 781938 463112